Betrayal of Trust

by London St. Charles

LS Publishing Group
Chicago, Illinois

LS Charles Publishing Group
www.londonstcharles.com

Betrayal of Trust by London St. Charles Copyright ©2019
Trade Paperback ISBN: 978-0-9993288-2-8
E-book ASIN: B07P687SBN

Cover Designed by:
J.L Woodson: www.woodsoncreativestudio.com
Interior Designed by: Lissa Woodson: www.naleighnakai.com
Editor: Lisa Watson: www.lisawatson.com

Dedication:

To my Bradley-Thomas Crew,
this one's for you!

Just because someone appears healthy and in control of their emotions on the outside, doesn't mean they aren't battling an internal struggle. Sometimes we forget to make sure the "resilient" and the "seems to have it all together person" is okay. Many times, those are the ones who need the most support but are afraid to ask for fear of looking weak or less than to the people who depend on them or by society's standards. It's okay NOT to be okay. You are loved. Always remember that.

—London St. Charles

Acknowledgements

Thank you, Father for giving me the gift to create and the know how to grind and utilize my vivid imagination. Through you all things are possible.

This project is near and dear to my heart. Thanks to all who've helped along this journey. Words of encouragement, sounding boards, venting sessions, character discussions, all of it, whether I took your advice or not, know that your input was not in vain and I appreciate your investment in the success of my work.

Tribe, thanks for always supporting your Sister Scribe, sharing my posts, reading excerpts, and sending positive vibes. Naleighna Kai, thanks for cultivating this group of amazingly talented authors. My writing life has been forever changed. To my editor, Lisa Watson, I love what you did with this story (that fairy dust we talked about lol), yeah, all of that! Thank you. To my beta readers who didn't hesitate to read my story when asked, J.D. Mason, Christine Pauls, MarZé Scott, Debra Mitchell, and Marva Harden, thanks for your critiques and honest feedback #swoon. My graphic designer, J.L. Woodson, this cover is boss.

My family and friends, thanks for always pushing me to tell my stories and supporting my writing career. I know I can get long-winded when I start talking about the story I'm working on. Thanks for sharing my enthusiasm and for giving it to me straight. I love you for life.

To the readers, YOU are who I do this for. Thanks for your continued support!

One Love,
London St. Charles

Chapter 1

"Who's there?" Cedrick Dalton whipped around, knocking the whiskey tumbler filled with Bourbon off the bar, along with dozens of receipt tabs.

"It's me, babe," said his wife, Sierra, jumping backward as the shards of glass ricocheted off the dark-stained hardwood floors. "I didn't mean to startle you."

"What are you doing——? How did you get in here?" he asked, sporadically turning while scanning the empty dining area.

"Juan let me in," she said pointing over her shoulder toward the entrance of The Smokehouse restaurant that Cedrick owned. "He was on his way out. What's with the third degree? It's not like I haven't dropped by after hours before."

Cedrick opened his mouth to respond just as the restaurant's phone rang. The galloping beat of his heart lunged into his throat, making it hard for him to speak.

"What's going on with you?" she asked, stepping over the glass. "I wanted to surprise you for dinner," she said lifting take-out bags from their favorite Japanese restaurant, placing them on the bar counter and claiming a seat. "Are you gonna get that?"

He hadn't planned on answering the phone. Who would be calling the restaurant after hours? All the workers were gone, and his wife was sitting in front of him, so it wasn't her. The best way to reach any staff was on the service line, but again, it was after closing.

Cedrick walked behind the bar, cleared his throat, then answered the phone. "Smokehouse." After a brief pause, he said, "Hello." Sighing and crossing his arms, he asked, "Who's there?"

A hard click, followed by a dial tone, resonated in his ear. That was the fourth phantom call this evening. Add that to the messages the hostess received earlier during the day that someone had been trying to reach him but wouldn't leave a name or a call back number made Cedrick officially paranoid.

After all, it was Halloween. Strange things had been known to happen on the devil's holiday as his father referred to it, but it was hard for Cedrick to accept that reasoning alone. It was also the anniversary of a day he'd been trying to forget since the age of fourteen. Guilt and fear haunted his soul every day, but especially on October thirty-first. *Is it a coincidence that the random occurrences are happening today?* He thought, placing the receiver on the base.

Sierra raised an eyebrow. "Tell that chick your wife's here and she has to wait her turn." She winked and giggled, removing the white boxes, packets of soy sauce, and chopsticks from the bag.

"She knows better," Cedrick teased with a forced smile, wishing it was that simple. He could deal with a secret admirer. At least they meant him no harm. The mystery person on the phone was a different story.

"Hand me a towel," Sierra said, sliding off the stool. "You don't want the wood to absorb any more of this liquor. It'll ruin the finish."

"Don't worry about that." Cedrick dismissed with the wave of a hand, glancing toward the entrance as he reached for the push broom. "I'll get it."

"Why do you keep checking the door?"

Cedrick averted his gaze and stroked his goatee. He felt Sierra's eyes blazing through him as though she could read his mind. She'd surely leave him if she knew what he'd done. Cedrick wouldn't be able to protect her if she did. It was a dead-end situation with no positive outcome.

"I'm ready to get out of here, that's all. Do you mind if we eat this at home?" he asked, hoping she'd say yes.

"I do," Sierra replied with a sassiness in her tone. "I was trying to do something spontaneous. I could've ordered take-out, left you a plate in the microwave, and been sleep when you finally made your way home, as usual. But I asked my mom to watch the girls, and I took the time to get cute, which you didn't even compliment me on," she chided crossing her legs at the ankles and doing a slow pirouette, showcasing the knee-high leather boots and a red-fitted sweater dress. "So yeah, I mind."

"Okay, sweetheart. Just give me a minute," he begged while cleaning the mess he made. Once Cedrick was done, he eased next to Sierra and stood directly in front of her. Caressing her rosy cheek and then lifting her chin, Cedrick didn't speak until she returned eye contact. "I appreciate you going out of your way to create a special evening for us, pretty lady. Thank you."

He walked behind the bar and grabbed two glasses from the overhead wineglass rack and a bottle of Red Moscato. The fruity aromas of wild cherry and peaches danced in the air as he filled their glasses half-way.

Solace crept into his aura while in Sierra's presence which temporarily took his mind off of his troubles and he was thankful. His beautiful wife was just what he needed.

"These noodles are extra tasty," Sierra said, grabbing them with her chopsticks and cupping her hand underneath, holding it to Cedrick's mouth.

"Mmmm," he moaned licking his lips. "I'd have to agree."

Twenty minutes into dinner and over three-fourths of the wine consumed, Cedrick asked, "What do you think about relocating?"

"To where?"

"Sunny Orlando."

"Why do you want to move to Florida?" Sierra asked, frowning. "Too many gators lurking on the lawn. Too many hurricanes and it's humid all the time. My natural hair would always stay poofy."

Cedrick let out a hearty laugh, even though he was dead serious. The more distance he put between his hometown of Reno, Nevada and his family, the better. Chicago had been a great city of refuge, but a change would be great.

"Orlando is pretty safe from hurricanes," he replied. Besides, the girls would love living that close to Disney World."

"And what about your restaurant? You're one of the hottest chefs on the Mag Mile," she countered. "You'd have to start over, and I know you don't want to do that. You can't be the head chef here and in Florida."

"My Sous Chef is more than capable of running the kitchen here," Cedrick countered, sipping the last of his drink.

"I'm sure Juan could handle it if he had to," Sierra remarked, gazing at Cedrick. "It sounds like you've given this some thought, and here I am thinking this was a hypothetical question."

"It was."

Sierra peered at him while biting into a sushi roll. "Maybe we could consider something like that when Carrington goes off to college," she said, holding her hand in front of her mouth as she munched on the rice, raw fish, and vegetables.

That's eight years from now. Cedrick thought, doing the math. He prayed his luck lasted that long for his family's sake.

Cedrick topped off Sierra's drink, then walked behind the bar to get a new bottle of wine. He wondered what she would think of him if she knew his truth. Would she understand that a moments decision changed the trajectory of his life? He'd give anything to not live in constant fear; to know that his family was protected.

"Did you hear that?" Cedrick asked Sierra, turning toward the swinging door that led to the kitchen. He felt the rapid pounding of his heart in his ears.

"I didn't hear anything," she responded, leaning forward.

"Someone's in there," he whispered, snatching a baseball bat from underneath the bar. "Stay put," he ordered, dashing to the side of the door, then peeked through the small window before slowly pushing it open.

"I'm surprised you're still here," a deep voice with an accent said from behind Sierra.

She shrieked, sending a chill down Cedrick's spine as he hopped the bar in one swoop with the bat clutched as if he were about to hit a home run.

"Whoa, boss. It's me." Juan jumped back.

"You scared the hell out of me," Sierra shouted, clenching her chest and sliding off the stool.

"What are you doing here?" Cedrick asked, inhaling a deep breath through his nostrils and exhaling through his mouth.

"I left my phone in my locker," Juan replied. "I called from my girlfriend's phone, but for some reason, I could hear you, but you couldn't hear me.

Cedrick's grip on the base of the bat eased a little. *That explained the last call, but what about the others?*

Juan left immediately after retrieving his phone. This time, Cedrick went to the door and locked it himself. He wanted to salvage what remained of the evening with his wife; unfortunately, his state of mind was right back where it was when Sierra arrived.

"Let's get out of here. I've had enough of this place for one evening," Cedrick said. "I'm off tomorrow morn——"

"Really? You haven't taken a Sunday off in ages."

"I'm only going in for the dinner rush, so I'm all yours until three." He winked, then tilted his head to the side. "How would you like to have brunch at Chef Brasseur's French Cuisine?"

"You know I love that place. I haven't been there since the remodel," Sierra beamed, and her smile warmed his conflicted interior.

"I have a meeting with Chef Brasseur, but once that's done, we can have a romantic brunch and spend the day together."

"I'd like that very much."

Sierra tossed the leftover food and wiped down the counter while Cedrick did a walk-thru in the kitchen. Juan may not have entered that way, but Cedrick still believed he heard movement in there. He needed to see for himself that everything was the way he left it, and of most importance, that the kitchen exit door was secured.

After a thorough once-over, Cedrick grabbed Sierra's hand and headed toward the exit. He set the alarm, then shut off the lights. "Thanks for your thoughtfulness tonight," Cedrick said, lifting her hand to his lips. "I love you."

"I love you, too, but we better get out of here before that alarm sounds," she teased. "You can *show* me how much you appreciate me when we get home."

"Lead the way."

Making love to his wife was a great way to take his mind off of things.

Cedrick pushed the door open and stepped to the side to allow Sierra to exit. Just as she crossed the threshold, the restaurant phone rang.

Chapter 2

Ten thousand swords stabbed Cedrick's body all at once. His breath hitched in his throat as he struggled to compose himself. It had been over fifteen years since he'd seen anyone from his hometown of Reno, Nevada. Yet here he was in a Chicago restaurant wondering if the woman sitting at the table across from him and Sierra would recognize him? His jaw clenched with dread.

"Excuse me," Sierra said, tapping the waiter's arm as he maneuvered between the tables. "Where's the ladies' room?"

The waiter pointed down the hall.

Cedrick pushed the gold-wired framed glasses up with an index finger, then stroked his goatee. A tense look crossed his face.

"Babe, what's wrong?" Sierra asked, standing and straightening her blouse.

"Nothing," he responded, continuing to stroke his goatee.

She narrowed her gaze on him. "You always do that when you're worried about something. Last night, and now today."

"I'm fine," he dismissed.

"We'll talk about it when I get back," Sierra said, touching Cedrick's hand, slowly removing it from his face before walking away.

Nothing got past this woman. She'd always been able to read him, especially his discomfort. There's only one other person who had that gift, and she sat at the next table.

Cedrick unrolled the silverware from the napkin, wiped the moisture from his brow, and opened the menu as he sunk into the seat, attempting to make his six-foot-five frame disappear. While checking emails on his phone, Cedrick peered over the menu to observe the woman he could never forget.

Victoria Weiss was his childhood friend with a unique patch of curly white hair that made her unmistakable. She had a laugh that could fill all the cavernous gaps in the universe, especially those from his tumultuous Muslim childhood.

"Sorry for the wait, Chef Cedrick," the hostess apologized, causing him to flinch and knock his phone to the floor. "Chef Brasseur will be right out."

"Thank you," he replied, leaning over to pick it up while fumbling to hold the menu in place to hide his face.

"No worries." The hostess stooped graciously with her knees together, retrieved the phone, and placed it on the table.

He nodded with a fleeting smile, rubbing his thumb and index finger across his goatee for the second time. His wife was right. He needed a different outlet for his anxiousness.

"You still do that when you're nervous, I see," the tender voice said with amusement from across the table. Her warm smile showed the beautiful imperfections God had embedded in her cinnamon cheeks. "I almost didn't recognize you sporting the Mr. Clean bald head and sculpted body. I see the years have been good to you."

Cedrick's chest expanded causing his ribs to hurt from the pressure. He was worried.

Victoria was no one's fool. Cedrick had shaved his locs the moment he and his mom fled Nevada and moved to Illinois. Apparently, maturity and a new appearance didn't mean anything to someone who knew him better than he knew himself.

Supermodel legs wrapped in plum leggings and high heeled, peep toe, belted ankle boots, strode toward his table. Cedrick had dreamt of seeing his longtime friend again, but he never thought it would actually happen.

"Uwezo Omari, you hear me talking to you," she said, standing at his table.

The sound of Cedrick's given name paralyzed him. He broke with the Muslim faith years ago. Now, he studied Christianity, had joined a Catholic Church, drank alcohol socially, had several tattoos, and ate pork. Cedrick even went as far as opening an upscale Smokehouse restaurant where he knew devout Muslims wouldn't dare enter, especially no one from his past. He thought he was safe.

"Boy, you better get up and give me a hug," Victoria demanded, placing hands on her hips.

Cedrick glanced over his shoulder toward the direction of the ladies' room, then back at Victoria.

"Don't fret. Your lady friend——"

"My wife," he corrected.

"No disrespect intended," she replied, holding her hands in the air. "Uwezo Oma——"

"Don't call me that." He rose, towering over Victoria's slender frame. "I go by Cedrick now."

"Whatever." She flung her arms around his neck. "I'm so happy to see you. Everyone back home thought you were either dead or in jail the way you vanished without a trace." She released him, dabbing the area under her bottom lashes to keep sudden moisture from ruining her eyeliner.

Cedrick's brow dampened, and the wetness under his armpits trickled down his sides. Thankfully, he was wearing a dark colored shirt.

The visual of his father lying in a pool of blood with a fork lodged in his neck, clasping the Quran flashed through his mind. Cedrick shook that horrifying memory aside. He glanced down at Victoria.

"And it must stay that way."

"I don't understa——"

"Don't tell anyone you saw me," Cedrick pleaded, gazing over his shoulder to make sure Sierra hadn't seen him with his old friend.

Other than Cedrick's mother, Priscilla, Sierra didn't know anyone from his life before he moved to Chicago, and he planned to keep it that way for both their safety.

"This must be the lovely Sierra," Chef Brasseur said with a smile brighter than The Bean in Millennium Park.

Cedrick wiped his clammy palms along his pants before shaking Chef Brasseur's hand. "No, this is my friend, Victoria. Sierra's indisposed at the moment, but she'll be right back."

"My apologies. *Bonjour ravie de vous rencontrer mademoiselle,*" Chef Brasseur greeted, kissing the back of her hand.

"Oh my." Victoria giggled.

Her laughter reminded Cedrick of the many times they'd played truth or dare. She'd always choose truth, then giggle because no one could make her do anything ridiculous. He had always thought playing with Victoria was unfair since she never picked a dare.

"It was nice seeing you, Vicki." Cedrick hoped she took the hint and retreated to her table. He wanted her to leave the restaurant, but since he wasn't in his own establishment, he didn't have any grounds to have her escorted off the premises.

Victoria swiped Cedrick's phone from the table and tapped the screen as if typing a text. He opened his mouth to speak just as her phone rang.

"There." She flipped the phone around. Victoria's number was splayed across the top of the screen. "I'll lock your number in, and you do the same with mine. Call me so we can catch up. I have so much to tell you about what's going on back home."

That's the last thing Cedrick wanted to hear.

Chef Brasseur glanced down at his wristwatch. "If you need a few minutes——"

A woman wearing a toque blanche hat and double-breasted jacket barreled out of the French kitchen doors.

"We have a situation," she whispered with a quivering voice over Chef Brasseur's shoulder.

"If you'll excuse me," Chef Brasseur said in a commanding tone.

"We can reschedule for another time," Cedrick suggested, catching a glimpse of Sierra heading their way. "I'll be in touch."

"*Merci,*" Chef Brasseur said, pivoting on his heels, rushing toward the kitchen with the Sous Chef in tow.

"Don't tell anyone you saw me," Cedrick mumbled loud enough for Victoria to hear, grabbing Sierra's cardigan from the back of the chair. "I'll call you when I can."

Victoria's brows furrowed. "What's going on with you?"

"I mean it ... you never saw me."

She took a seat as Sierra walked up behind Cedrick. "Sorry I took so long," she said glancing in Victoria's direction. "The lines in the ladies' room were crazy."

After a slight pause and a questioning glare, Sierra asked, "Do I know you?"

Cedrick's heart jolted. He wanted to disappear in the kitchen with Chef Brasseur.

"I don't believe so," Victoria replied.

"Then why were you chatting with my husband while I was gone? Are you one of these food-obsessed-Instagram chef groupies?"

Cedrick eyeballed Victoria and gave a warning frown before turning his back on her and facing his wife.

"Sierra—— let's not do this," Cedrick stated, holding up the cardigan so she could slide her arms inside the sleeves. "Chef Brasseur had an emergency. We're going to meet at another time."

"Who is she?"

"A patron of this restaurant."

"I'm tired of these fangirls." Sierra pursed her shimmery-bronzed colored lips.

This was one-time Cedrick's local celebrity played in his favor.

"I'm begging you, please don't cause a scene. I'm trying to woo

Chef Brasseur to come work for me. You confronting one of his customers is not a good look."

Sierra ignored her husband's warning. She leaned over Victoria's table and hissed, "I'm watching you."

Victoria snickered. "I hope you like what you see."

Sierra reared back into a defensive stance.

All eyes and cell phones were on them.

Cedrick wrapped his arm around Sierra's waist and ushered her out of the restaurant before she had a chance to utter another word or do something they'd both regret.

Chapter 3

Sierra slid in the passenger's seat and whipped out her phone. Opening Instagram, she searched *Smokehouse_Chef* to see if the woman she'd seen in the restaurant was one of Cedrick's followers. Something about her seemed familiar. It was unsettling.

Women salivated over Cedrick like he was the tender beef brisket he marinated, smoked, and served in his restaurant. They'd ask for her husband's autograph or a selfie in her presence while apologizing for interrupting their outing. Sierra was accustomed to that, but to wait until she left the room, that was uncalled for sneakiness, and it got her hackles up.

Turning to Sierra, Cedrick asked, "We have the rest of the afternoon free, sweetheart. Any ideas?"

She pondered the question as he maneuvered the Dodge Charger out of the parking garage. Despite the light tone he used, Sierra couldn't keep the edge out of her voice at not finding the woman she searched for amongst his followers. "Take me to the office."

Cedrick sighed aloud. "On a Sunday? Come on, Sierra. This is the first afternoon I've had off in months, and you want to spend it at the office?"

"I won't be long," she promised, rubbing a hand along the side of her smoothly tapered curly afro. "We're right down the street. I need to go over the files for the Eastside Development Project one last time before we meet with the client tomorrow. I'll only be a couple of hours."

"That's all I have is a couple of hours before the dinner rush surges," he shot back. "You know I'm the only joint open late on Sundays in the area. I need to get back there before it gets crazy."

Sierra sighed. She wanted to spend the afternoon with her husband, but this had to be done. Had Cedrick not rushed her out of the restaurant, they could've enjoyed some quality time together, but now she was pressed for time, especially with her mother watching their kids for the day.

"You don't even have your work bag."

She patted the oversized Burberry leather tote. "Everything I need's in here."

"So, you already had this planned," Cedrick pouted, swerving into the taxi lane of the mirrored skyscraper.

"Babe, of course not, but my work is just as demanding as yours," she reminded him. "The only difference now is that you're here feeling what I go through every morning."

Cedrick put the car in park and turned to his wife. "Meaning what?"

"Come on, Cedrick," she replied with exasperation. "You leave every day at the crack of dawn and don't return home until after the kids, and I have gone to bed."

His expression grew pained. "Sierra, it's not——"

"Shhhh." She pressed a finger to his full lips. "I didn't say that to make you feel bad. I just want you to understand that it goes both ways." She plucked a keycard and ID from her tote. "Go get Carrington and Lena from mom. Hang out at Navy Pier for a few hours. It's not too cold for a Ferris wheel ride. They'll love that." She grabbed the handle. "I'll catch an Uber home, get my car and meet you to pick them up."

"Okay, but I miss you, Sierra." Cedrick caressed her cheek and leaned in, placing a soft kiss on her lips.

Sierra inhaled his sweet woody scent, a stark contrast to the smoky aroma that usually flanked his clothes and body. She almost changed her mind. Almost.

"I miss you too. I'll wait up for you," Sierra promised, sliding a hand over his thigh before floating out of the car.

* * *

Cedrick put on the hazard lights, hopped out the car, and fell in-step with Sierra. "I want to make sure you get into the building okay."

"Always the gentleman." She smiled, swiping her keycard, punching a code in the keypad, then leaning over a screen that scanned her irises. A few seconds later, the red button on the keypad flashed green, and the glass door clicked open.

Cedrick held the handle, permitting his wife to enter. "Text me when you make it upstairs."

"Will do."

"You make sure she's alright," Cedrick said to the security guard sitting behind the desk.

He sat in his car, awaiting Sierra's confirmation. Besides wanting to spend the day with her, Cedrick didn't like Sierra being in the office alone. It was only a few weeks ago that she told him that one of her colleagues had been assaulted in the ladies' room while working overtime on the weekend and the perpetrator was still at large.

Once Sierra texted, Cedrick made a U-turn, heading to his mother-in-law's house to get the girls. He got caught by the red light, directly in front of Chef Brasseur's restaurant. Gazing at the marquee, he couldn't help but wonder why Victoria was in town? Did she know the *real* reason he left Reno?

He drove a couple of blocks, then pulled over. Curiosity got the better of him. He needed to know why Victoria was in Chicago. His life and the ones he loved, lives depended on it.

Only thirty minutes had passed since he'd left the restaurant. There was a chance that Victoria was still there, so Cedrick called the last number dialed on his phone. Victoria answered on the first ring.

"Are you still at the restaurant?" he asked before she could say hello.

"Yes."

"Meet me outside in two minutes," he said, checking the side mirror for oncoming traffic before pulling away from the curb. "I'm in a black Dodge Charger with tinted windows."

After disconnecting the call, Cedrick tried to focus on driving, but it was difficult. The whole afternoon had been upturned. He'd gone through the full gamut of emotions since Victoria sidled up to his table earlier. Shock, dismay, worry, and fear were just a few. Now there was some tension between him and his wife because of Victoria's inopportune drop-in.

Unable to help himself, his mind wandered back to his old life with his best friend. The goodbye kiss Cedrick planted on her lips fifteen years ago should've never happened, but if he had to have his first kiss with anyone, he was glad it was with Vicki, regardless of the circumstances.

"What's up?" she asked, sliding into the car. "You can imagine how surprised I am to hear from you so soon. Earlier, you treated me like I had Ebola or something."

Cedrick's hands trembled. His expression darkened.

"Uwezo." She grinned, laying her purse into her lap. "It was a joke."

His features didn't soften. That name. The past. All bad vibes.

"This isn't a good idea, Vicki." He cranked the engine. "I think you should go."

She touched his shoulder. "Hold up, Uwezo."

Cedrick shook her hand off.

"I mean, Cedrick," Victoria corrected. "You've got to tell me what's going on with you. I haven't seen or heard from you since you ghosted me years ago. I asked your mother where you were, and she told me you were at your Aunt Makayla's house. Then I freaked out when you didn't show up to school the next day, or the next. Didn't I mean anything to you?"

"You know better than to ask that," he cautioned.

"Then I suggest you start talking because you owe me an explanation Uw—Cedrick."

Cedrick closed his eyes.

Victoria whispered, "You not coming to school didn't make sense. Education was everything to you. Even after your dad broke your foot and refused to take you for medical treatment until you studied the Quran, you hobbled to school in a makeshift cast." She batted the tears away. "So, after you missed a few days, I came by after school to check on you— the house was empty, and the car was gone." Her voice broke, and tears came in earnest.

Cedrick thought about that memory. That one incident alone was what caused him to swear he'd never force religion on his girls. They had the right to choose their path. His job was to raise well-rounded, kind-spirited, respectful children who knew right from wrong. He'd like to think that thus far, he and Sierra had accomplished that.

He eyed Victoria. "Why are you here in Chicago?"

She reared back in her seat. "After everything, I just said— that's your response?"

"Look, I don't need a tour guide down memory lane to be reminded of all the bad things that happened to me."

"Whoa," Victoria remarked, shifting in the seat, leaning closer to Cedrick. "This is me ... the one who traveled that dark road with you. The only friend you trusted with your truth. I'm still that person."

That's the problem. Cedrick couldn't trust it. He loved Victoria more than she would ever know. Because of her friendship and the fact that she kept his secrets, he had the strength to get out of an abusive situation. But her father was a cop. Cedrick couldn't chance coming clean to her. Not now. Not ever.

"I want to believe you."

A rapid tap on the driver's window by a policeman alarmed Cedrick. Fear catapulted into his stomach causing it to clench in knots. Whenever he grew worried, his digestion system was the first to suffer. Right now, his nerves were stretched so taut he felt he'd lose his bowels if he weren't careful.

She set me up.

Cedrick glared at Victoria as his worst fears came to light. His best friend, the keeper of his painful secrets had betrayed him. The past had finally caught up at the hands of his most trusted friend. Images of his wife, mother, and kids visiting him in jail through a thick glass panel made his eyes water.

The officer tapped again, this time a little harder. Cedrick reluctantly lowered the window. At that moment, the Sahara Desert had more moisture than his mouth.

"Yes, officer."

"Move your car. Now. You're in a loading zone."

"Sorry," he replied with relief and prayed the officer didn't notice his anxiousness.

Cedrick hadn't been this jumpy in years. One glimpse of Victoria and he was fourteen again—— weak and afraid.

"I have to go," Cedrick said to Victoria, putting the gear in drive.

"Wait, I'm not leaving," she countered, fastening the seatbelt. "You'd better move before Officer Friendly gives you a ticket," she teased in a tone not matching the joking banter.

Cedrick's face echoed the exasperation he felt at her stubbornness. He mumbled under his breath but still drove a few streets over, down Columbus Drive, and parked across the street from Buckingham Fountain. The meters were free on Sundays, so they had time to talk without interruptions.

"Okay, you aren't getting a ticket, we're parked and in no immediate danger. So please quit stalling and tell me what the heck's going on with you?" Victoria poked Cedrick in the arm as she spoke and didn't stop until he returned eye contact. "Fifteen years ago, you asked me to forgive you. I thought you were talking about the kiss." She hesitated. "But now, I think it's about something else."

"Why do you keep questioning me?"

"Because my best friend disappeared from my life almost two decades ago and by the grace of God, I ran into him today. I deserve answers," she cried out, her voice breathy and filled with emotion. "Where've you been all this time? Why didn't you reach out to me? My life fell apart after you left. I needed you—— and you weren't there."

Unable to continue, Victoria turned toward the window.

Cedrick stared in disbelief as she struggled to pull herself together. Her emotional outburst gave him pause. Not once had he ever considered the impact that his absence would have on Victoria.

Every raised fist, every hurled object, every broken bone, all in the name of Allah—— it disgusted him.

He never understood why his father disliked him so much, initially thinking he was being disciplined for bad behavior. During the early years of suffering, Cedrick witnessed the overt pleasure his dad displayed at hurting him. It was in his eyes the first time his father fractured his wrist. Cedrick's cry for help was met with a violent shove to the floor and a throaty laugh. He knew then that his father and Lucifer were well acquainted.

Beaten and damaged, after that incident, Cedrick refused to let his father have the satisfaction of seeing him whimper. He'd never made that mistake again.

"Earth to Cedrick." Victoria snapped her fingers in his face.

Blinking out of the trance, Cedrick gripped the steering wheel so tight that his knuckles protruded. "So much has happened—— I can't talk about it," he muttered. "Believe me. I would if I could, Vicki."

"I don't know what you're so afraid to tell me. You used to tell me everything," Victoria reminded Cedrick, leaning toward him. "But if it'll ease your mind—— I'm in town on business. My father-in-law's a partner at a big-time law firm here in Chicago. I'm the architectural engineer on the deal he's closing with Eastside Development Project and——"

"Eastside Development with Smithe, Banks, & Wilkerson Attorneys at Law?" Cedrick's voiced hitched, at the mention of the law firm that Sierra worked at for six years.

Victoria's eyes widened. "Yeah. How did you know?"

Chapter 4

"Mommy, the garage is on fire," Carrington screamed, peering through the yellow sheer kitchen curtain that adorned the window that faced the backyard. The remnants of milk and Honey Nut Cheerios dripped from her mouth onto her maroon uniform shirt. "Mommy," she yelled, running toward her baby sister, Lena's bedroom.

Sierra appeared in the doorway with Lena on her hip. "Fire," her mother repeated with a questioning arch of an eyebrow. "This had better not be another one of your jokes," she warned walking down the short hall, then into the kitchen. "We're already running late. Did you finish your breakfast?"

"No. Mommy." Carrington whipped her head, and her golden-brown shoulder blade length hair followed. "I'm not joking. There's smoke coming from under the garage."

Sierra ran to the kitchen window, swiping the curtain to the side almost pulling the rod from the frame. "Sweet Jesus." She gasped, kicking off a pair of black heels and shoving nine-month-old Lena into Carrington's arms. "Call 9-1-1," Sierra shouted, rushing down the small flight of stairs that led to the back door. "Wait by the front door. Don't move from that spot until the firemen arrive."

"Okay, Mommy." She froze, frightened by the roughness of her mother's tone.

The heebie-jeebies took over her insides, threatening to turn the contents in her stomach into a gushing geyser. That made her frown. She didn't want vomit all over her uniform shirt.

The loud slam of the screen door smacking the frame snapped Carrington out of the trance.

"Phone," she whispered, whirling around while fear made her heart beat to the rhythm of conga drums. Carrington's eyes zeroed in on the charging dock on the kitchen counter. Her phone wasn't there, but it should've been. She placed it on the dock at seven thirty. That was the rule on school nights.

She searched along the floor and inside the cabinets. Where could her phone have gone?

Securely holding onto a squirming Lena, Carrington sprinted down the hall and entered her bedroom. *Carrington's Purple Palace* was stenciled with various hues of purple rhinestones on the white-paneled door. She slid a hand with multicolored nail polish under a pillow, but the phone wasn't there. That's usually where Carrington hid it when she seized the rare opportunity to talk on the phone, the nights her mother went to bed early. She'd always set the alarm as a reminder to return it before her mother stirred the following morning.

"Where is it?" She hiked Lena up on her side. Carrington tossed the purple comforter and sheets with white polka dots, completely stripping the bed. The phone wasn't there.

"Shoot. Shoot. Shoot," Carrington yelled, lifting her leg and pounding her foot into the carpet several times until she spotted the unicorn backpack sitting atop the white desk. She hit herself on the forehead and rolled her eyes. "Duh."

Placing Lena on the plush lavender carpet, she yanked every book, folder, and piece of paper out her backpack until she reached the phone tucked in the bottom. How could she forget getting busted by her dad last night when he peeked in the room to check on her after he got home from work? He took the phone and dropped it in her backpack.

Carrington punched the home screen button several times, but the phone did not turn on. The one time she didn't follow the rules, she really wished she had. Carrington jumped to her feet and dashed into her parent's room, searching for her mom's cell phone. She rumbled on top of and through the nightstand, vanity, and chest of drawers, but couldn't find it anywhere. And she couldn't call her mom's phone to hear it ring because her phone was dead. The consequences of her misbehavior were starting to add up.

"Aghhhhhhh," she screamed, throwing the phone down and pulling her hair.

Carrington didn't know what to do. Her mom hadn't come back inside, and she couldn't help her. What if she died in the fire? What if the fire spread to the house? Her daddy would never forgive her. It would be all her fault because she didn't listen.

Warm liquid trickled down Carrington's inner thighs and legs, soaking her ribbed white school tights.

Glancing down in shock at the yellowish stain, she caught a glimpse of Lena gumming her blue homework folder.

"No, Lena," she yelled, snatching the folder from her sister's mouth and tossed it on the bed. "You can't eat that."

"Bluuuuuuu." Lena blew raspberries, spraying Carrington's creamy cheeks with unwanted saliva.

"Ugh, Lena," she whined wiping her face and picking up the phone. "That's nasty."

Carrington shook the phone, then pressed the power button again. Nothing.

Tears welled in her bottom lids.

"Think Carrington, think," she chanted, hitting her temple with her fist. "What would mom do?" she whispered to herself, walking in a circle.

After a brief silence, she leaped in the air and shouted, "Oh my gosh."

Carrington darted out of her parent's bedroom to put the phone on the charging dock, but she tripped over Lena who had crawled out into the hallway. Carrington landed on her stomach, and her chin smacked the hardwood floor. Pain radiated from her mouth to her belly button, but she couldn't allow herself to wallow in agony. Her mom was counting on her.

Lena's piercing scream numbed all of Carrington's aches and blessed her with a new source of throbbing pain in her ears. Hopefully, Lena was startled from the noise of the fall and wasn't hurt from Carrington's foot kicking her belly when she tripped. She peeled herself off the floor and slammed the phone in the cradle. While waiting for the phone to power on, Carrington scooped Lena in her arms and ran as fast as she could muster to the kitchen window. Lena squeezed her chin and Carrington grabbed her by the wrist. She didn't realize she'd been bleeding until she saw Lena's little red streaked fingers.

Carrington glanced out the window and didn't see her mom anywhere. "Mommy," she squealed, causing Lena to perfect her soprano voice even louder, matching her sister's desperate cry.

She wiped her chin with the sleeve of her uniform shirt and swiftly took Lena into her bedroom. Carrington placed Lena in the chestnut crib and turned on Sesame Street. Lena continued to wail as her sister left the room.

Carrington dashed back into the kitchen. A picture of a battery with a red mark appeared on the phone screen. Tears of relief streaked Carrington's cheeks as she dialed 9-1-1, but the phone died soon as the operator said, "9-1-1, what's your emergency?"

"Noooooooo!" Carrington shrieked, sprinting out the back door.

She promised God that she would never disobey her mother ever again if He'd let her live.

Chapter 5

Sierra coughed, choking on the overwhelming intake of exhaust fumes from Cedrick's car inside the closed garage.

"Cedrick," she croaked while covering her mouth and nose with the sleeve of her navy suit jacket. Sierra slammed her fist against the gray button along the wall that automatically lifted the overhead garage door. "Cedrick."

She stuck her head out the side door of the garage, which was closest to her, filled her lungs with cold air, then ducked back inside. Sierra scooted behind Cedrick's car in an attempt to get to the driver's door, stubbing her big toe on something cold and hard. "Mmm," she moaned, swiping the object aside with her foot and tripping over a thick tube and falling to the ground, her pencil skirt ripping under the strain.

Sierra grabbed the rubbery object, pulling it closer to see what it was, but when she did, the fumes shot in her face, filling her nostrils and burning her eyes. Still holding the object, she crawled to the side door gasping for air for a second time. Her flesh-tone stockings frayed with every movement. She gulped in fresh air greedily, her lungs expanding and retracting deeply to ensure she cleared the poison from her body.

Getting to her feet, Sierra took a long deep breath, then rushed back into the garage. She slid behind Cedrick's car, then between her vehicle and his to get to the driver's door. The other end of the garden hose was wedged, and duck taped into the window. The life-threatening fumes were thick and suffocating.

Sierra yanked on the door handle, but it was locked. "Cedrick," she called out, looking around for anything she could use to break the window. "Hang on."

At that moment, a gust of frigid Chicago air whipped through the garage like a tornado. The cold air blasted over her stockinged feet, and her tattered clothes, but she was oblivious. As the atmosphere cleared, Sierra banged on the window with her fists. When he didn't respond, she yelled, "Carrington called 9-1-1. Help's on the way."

"What's wrong with Daddy?" Carrington asked, coughing.

Sierra's head snapped in the direction of her daughter's voice. Carrington was about to come into the garage.

"Carrington stop," she commanded. "Don't come in. It's not safe."

"Then why are you in there? What's wrong with Daddy?" Carrington cried, stepping inside.

"Something happened to Daddy's car. You need to get—" She grimaced. "What happened to your face?"

"I fell," she replied, holding her throat while coughing. "I'm okay."

Sierra took a second to register that her daughter was fine, then went back to barking orders.

"Carrington. Run down to Mr. Little's house and see if he or anyone else is out there," she instructed, clearing her throat.

Mr. Little was their neighbor who lived three houses over. He swept the sidewalk and curb every morning before walking to the café to grab a cup of coffee.

"If he's there, ask him to bring a hammer, a crowbar, or whatever. I need to break the window."

"Okay, Mommy," she responded. "But we got a hammer right here."

"Bring it to me, baby."

Carrington handed Sierra the wooden tool with the large steelhead.

"I have to stay here with Daddy until help arrives," Sierra said, rearing back and slamming the hammer into the window, sending pieces of glass flying everywhere. Pulling the door open, she reached over Cedrick's limp body and turned off the ignition. "You go back in and stay with Lena. When the fireman arrive, I need you to tell them we're out here."

"But Mommy——"

"No arguments, Carrington. Get moving."

"I ... I couldn't call them."

"What'd you mean?" Sierra barked harsher than intended.

"My phone—— is dead and—— I couldn't find yours," Carrington confessed.

"Dear God," she uttered, glancing down at her husband's lifeless body.

"Carrington, my phone's in my purse on the table by the front door. I need you to call them immediately and tell them we need an ambulance. Give them our address. If they need any other information, bring the phone to me." She eyed her daughter. "Can you do that?"

"Yes Mommy," Carrington said stoically before turning on her heels and bolting back into the house.

The moment her daughter left, Sierra turned her attention back to Cedrick. He was barely breathing but hadn't regained consciousness. "Cedrick," Sierra yelled, tapping his cheek with vigor. "Wake-up."

The fumes had dissipated, and the air around them was clean.

"C'mon baby, I need you to wake-up," she pleaded again.

Sierra could accept a mistake, but this she didn't understand. Why would Cedrick try to commit suicide? It didn't make any sense.

She lifted his eyelid but then shrieked with shock as her mother's ringtone permeated the air. Her phone had been tucked in her bra the entire time.

Sierra sent her mom to voicemail and dialed 9-1-1.

Moments later, Carrington rushed into the garage. She bent over to rest her hands on her knees as she huffed. "I can't find it, Mommy. Your phone's not there."

"It's okay." Sierra lifted her phone. "The ambulance is on the way." She rested a hand on Carrington's shoulder. "But we're going to have to get daddy out of here. He needs to get fresh air into his lungs."

Carrington's eyes widen to the size of tambourines. The fear was unmistakable.

"We can do it, baby," Sierra assured her daughter. "Get in on the other side and push Daddy toward me," she instructed. "Be careful of the glass."

A sleeping, soothing sound hummed in the distance, followed by crunching and grinding. "Stay here, honey. I'll be right back." Sierra hurried to the alley. The streets and sanitation truck were two houses down.

"Hey," Sierra yelled, flagging down the garbage man. She was sure he couldn't hear her over the noise of the compactor, but the driver saw her and hopped out of the cab.

Sierra ran toward the man in denim jeans and a bright yellow vest with silver reflective tape.

"Ma'am are you alright?" he asked glancing down at her feet. "You're bleeding."

"My husband's unconscious and I need your help. Please," she begged. "He's slumped over in his car." She pointed toward the garage. "And I can't get him out. He's inhaled a lot of carbon monoxide."

The man ran to the back of the garbage truck, and a second later, he was accompanied by two co-workers.

"This way." She ran with the men on her heels.

"Are you going to help my Daddy?" Carrington asked with tears in her eyes.

"We're going to do our best." He smiled. "My name's Rick."

"Please help him."

"We got him." He nodded. "Don't you worry about a thing."

Sierra grabbed Carrington and moved to the side. She clung to her daughter and prayed in silence for grace and mercy. A faint siren whistled in the wind, and she whispered, "Amen."

The men maneuvered Cedrick's body, sliding him out of the car and carrying him past the entryway of the garage and onto the concrete.

"Baby girl, could you get that piece of cardboard over there?" Rick asked, pointing in the direction of the lawn mower and snow blower.

Carrington tore from her mother's arms and brought it forward.

"Lay it right there," Rick directed.

She positioned the oversized piece of cardboard that her Daddy used when he worked underneath his car where she was told; then they laid him down on top of it.

"Daddy," Carrington cried, "Please don't die."

Sierra wrapped her arms around her baby and stroked her hair. "Daddy's going to be with us for a very long time. He's just exhausted from working so much; that's all."

"You promise?" Carrington asked, squeezing Sierra's small middle.

God doesn't give us more than we can handle. And he knows that I'm not ready to be a widow. "I promise." Sierra kissed Carrington's forehead. "Go inside and check on Lena. Stay with your sister."

The screeching siren of the ambulance entering the opposite end of the alley was welcoming. Sierra flexed her fingers as she released the breath she wasn't aware she'd been holding.

"Over here," Rick shouted, waving his arms frantically.

"Go on, Carrington. Daddy's going to be alright. The paramedics are here now." She squatted to get eye level with her daughter. Sierra held Carrington's hands and softly massaged them. "I need you to be a big girl and take care of Lena so that I can take care of Daddy, okay?"

Carrington nodded, then slowly walked toward the back door. The moment she was inside, Sierra rushed to Cedrick. She hovered anxiously over the female paramedic's shoulder. "Please tell me my husband's going to make it."

"He's not breathing," said the freckle-faced female paramedic to the male paramedic, while sliding her middle and index fingers in the groove of Cedrick's neck. After a few seconds, she announced, "He doesn't have a pulse."

"What? No," Sierra cried. "He was breathing moments ago, I checked."

She tried to rush toward Cedrick, but one of the sanitation workers grabbed her arm.

"It's okay, Miss. Just let them do what they can for your husband," he said quietly.

Frantic, Sierra stood by horrified while the emergency crew worked on her husband.

"We need to intubate," the man declared grabbing a round silver object and a clear tube. He inserted the tube in Cedrick's mouth and down his throat. "His airway's clear," the paramedic said. He then screwed a blue balloon-like ball to the end of the tube and squeezed it in even intervals.

Sierra's hands drew to her mouth and liquid pooled at the bottom of her eyelids.

The female paramedic opened Cedrick's coat, then cut his white chef uniform up the middle, exposing his broad chest. She then laced her fingers together and administered rapid chest compressions.

"I got the machine," the male paramedic mentioned as he pulled the protective tape off the adhesive defibrillation pads. His voice was steady but soothing. He applied one above the right nipple and the other on the left side below the breast area. "Shocking at 200. Clear."

Both paramedics lifted their hands and stepped away from Cedrick's body. His chest jerked forward, but he still wasn't breathing.

The female paramedic checked his pulse and repeated chest compressions.

Rick removed his work jacket, anchoring it around Sierra's shoulders. "He's going to be okay."

She wrapped her arms around herself and rocked back and forth.

"Charging to 300. Clear," the male paramedic announced, pushing the button on the machine to send another electric shock through Cedrick's body.

The machine beeped, and the female paramedic rechecked his neck. "I got a pulse. It's weak, but it's there."

"Thank God." Sierra allowed the tears of answered prayers to flow freely.

"What's your husband's name?" the female paramedic asked.

"Cedrick."

Placing a cervical collar around his neck, she asked, "Cedrick. Can you hear me?"

His eyes flew open and darted about the area. He reached for the tube stuck in his mouth, but the male paramedic grabbed his hands. "I can't let you do that," he warned.

"Can you tell me what happened?" the woman asked while assisting her partner putting Cedrick on a stretcher.

"I think he fell asleep with the car running." Sierra paused. "He works long hours."

She wouldn't dare tell them he tried to commit suicide. She was thankful now that she'd ripped the hose from the car's exhaust pipe.

"Do you know how long he's been exposed to carbon monoxide?"

"I'm not sure," she admitted, twirling her thumbs.

"He's fortunate you were here, ma'am," the female paramedic said, lifting the end of the stretcher into the rear of the ambulance. "Let me check you out."

"No, no, I'm fine," Sierra insisted, waving her off. "Just make sure he's okay."

"Be careful. Those lacerations could get infected." She pointed to Sierra's blood-stained feet. "Removing glass can be tricky."

Sierra nodded.

"We're taking him to Northwestern Hospital." The paramedic climbed into the back of the ambulance with Cedrick. "You can meet us there," she advised before closing the door.

The siren sounded causing Sierra to flinch. Flashing red lights spun above the ambulance as it zoomed down the alley. She watched until it was out of sight. Frozen in place, she closed her eyes and prayed for continued blessings.

Firm, thick fingers landed on her shoulders, disrupting her conversation with God.

"He's going to be alright," Rick said in a comforting tone.

"I know," Sierra replied, sliding the jacket off and handing it to him. "Thanks for your help, Rick." She glanced over at the other two men who were sweeping the glass with push brooms they'd found in the garage. "Without you guys—— this may have been a very different outcome."

Chapter 6

"Thanks, mom for grabbing the girls. I don't know what I'd do without you," Sierra whispered into the phone approaching the front desk of Northwestern Hospital's emergency department. "I'll keep you posted."

"Hi. I'm Sierra Dalton," she blurted hastily. "My husband, Cedrick Dalton was brought in by ambulance within the last twenty minutes." She pulled her identification and insurance cards from her purse. And—"

"One moment, Ms. Dalton," the intake nurse said, picking up the phone.

"Coming through," a high-pitched voice shouted.

Sierra turned to see what the commotion was all about when the man standing behind her stepped forward and coughed in her face.

"You. Have. *Got.* To be kidding me." She reached inside her purse and retrieved a baby wipe to clean the foreign germs away from her skin.

"I'm sorry, Miss—" the man fumbled.

"Excuse me, folks, I need more room," the paramedic pleaded, pushing a pregnant woman in a wheelchair through the congested area.

Sierra stepped to the side, pumped the hand sanitizer dispenser, and rubbed her hands together with vigor. She then plucked two blue cotton masks from the box on the counter. After securing one over her mouth and nose, she dangled the other one in front of the man.

"Thank you." He accepted the mask and put it on. "My apologies."

"Ms. Dalton," the nurse called. "Please step this way. Elise will take you back."

"What about the insurance?"

"Don't worry. The admissions representative will come to your husband's room to get it."

* * *

"Where is he?" Sierra spun around after eyeing the empty bed. Without anyone there, the patient room was cold and sterile. She tried to keep the fear from creeping up her spine as she waited for an answer.

"The tech took him down for some tests," Elise informed her. "He'll be back shortly." She offered a comforting smile before leaving Sierra alone.

She eased into a metal chair with a tan cushion, wringing her clear polished, manicured hands. Why would Cedrick try to commit suicide? Sierra couldn't wrap her mind around that no matter how hard she tried.

His restaurant was flourishing. He'd been in the black for three consecutive years, which allowed him to save a substantial amount of money. Sierra was the personal assistant to Edward Banks, one of the partners at Smithe, Banks, & Wilkerson Attorneys at Law. It was one of the largest real estate firms in the Midwest.

They bought their beautiful four-bedroom dream home in Lincoln Park during the foreclosure crisis for half of its worth, without having to finance it. Carrington attended the top Fine Arts school in the state, Lena's well cared for, and all other expenses were covered with ease. They were winning at living the American dream.

Sierra ran a hand absentmindedly through her hair. It didn't make sense. Money was the top reason for suicide among men. What other reason could he have for trying to kill himself?

The ringing phone tore Sierra from her thoughts. She plucked it from her pocket. SB&W flashed at the top of the screen. "Darn it." She sucked her teeth, then put on her professional voice.

"Good morning, Edward," Sierra greeted. "My apologies for not calling. I had a family emergency that required my presence."

"Where are the notes for today's meeting with Phil Archibald of Eastside Development?"

He could at least act like he's concerned.

"On my desk in the manila file folder labeled, EDP."

"I'm at your desk, Sierra." He paused.

She listened to the shuffling of papers on the other end of the receiver. Edward didn't have to ransack her desk. The folder was on top of the pile in the left-hand corner. Sierra made sure she'd arranged everything in order of importance while in the office on Sunday. Property values along the lakefront, the accounting, offers from competitors, and possible revenue from tourist were all calculated. Millions of dollars were on the table.

"The only thing in this folder is your daughter's school work," he barked.

That's not possible. Or is it? Could she had grabbed the wrong folder?

Sierra yanked two manila folders from her tote. One had property listings for a client in the Evanston area. The second one had the Eastside Development Project files.

Tico Torres of Bon Jovi couldn't have beat his drum harder or faster than the violent thrashing of her heart. She was about to blow the biggest project the firm had ever landed and lose her job in the process. Things couldn't possibly be any worse.

"Look who's here," the short orderly in light blue scrubs with snoopy designs said, wheeling Cedrick into the room.

Sierra's smile didn't quite meet her eyes, but that had nothing to do with her husband.

"The doctor will be in shortly," the orderly informed them, folding the footrest so Cedrick could stand.

"Thank you," she mouthed.

"I don't know what you've got going on, and frankly, I don't care," Edward growled.

It's worse. Sierra thought, closing her eyes in defeat.

"Phil will be here at ten. You better make it happen."

"Edward——"

The call abruptly disconnected.

Shaking harder than a dope fiend having withdrawals, Sierra stood, placing the phone on the edge of the sink. She struggled to compose herself. Pasting a warm smile on her face, she walked over to her husband's bed and sat at his side.

"Hi," she said in as neutral a tone as she could muster.

Cedrick jumped right in. "I'm sorry I scared you," he mumbled with his head bowed.

Sierra laid a hand across the soft cotton fabric of the hospital gown and caressed his chest. The feel of his heart pumping beneath her palm calmed her. They had experienced too close of a call.

"Cedrick." She stroked his bruised cheek with care.

He glanced upward, and she gazed into his troubled orbs.

"We have to talk."

"I know," he responded as the automatic blood pressure cuff inflated, holding his upper arm hostage before beeping and deflating again.

"But—— I have to go," she stated in a regretful tone.

"I understand if you can't stand the sight of me right now."

"Honey, why would you say that?" She shifted on the bed and

traced his arched eyebrow with her thumb. "I'm thankful you're alright. That you're here. We'll get through this, but—— the Eastside Development representatives are on the way to the firm and I have to get the paperwork to Edward," Sierra explained in a sad tone. "Or else I won't have a job."

"Then you need to go," Cedrick replied, grabbing the bedrail, gasping for air. His chest rose and fell at quick, uneven intervals.

"What's happening?" Sierra asked as the heart monitor beeped faster, and the numbers jumped all over the screen.

She pushed the call button, then placed her hand over his. "I need a nurse in here," Sierra shouted, staring into Cedrick's dilated pupils. "Breathe, baby."

"What happened?" the nurse asked, whisking the privacy drape aside, sticking the probes of the stethoscope in her ears.

"Nothing," Sierra responded, reading the nurse's name badge. "We were talking, and then he began to gasp like he isn't getting any air."

"Did you say something to upset him?" Nurse Deidre inquired.

"No—— I don't know—— Maybe," Sierra cupped her hands and blew air into them. "Not intentionally."

"Cedrick, focus on me, alright," the nurse instructed. "You're not in any danger, okay. You're having a panic attack."

His eyes widened and were transfixed on his wife.

"Are you sure?" Sierra questioned. "He's never had a panic attack before."

"This is what it appears to be," the nurse countered, then spoke to Cedrick. "Purse your lips together. Then I want you to take a deep breath in through your nose and exhale slowly from your mouth."

"C'mon honey," Sierra encouraged. "I'll do it with you," she said, placing a loving touch to his forearm.

"That's it, Cedrick." Nurse Deidre gave him two thumbs up.

After several repetitions, his breathing slowed. Sierra watched as it became regular and steady.

"We're still waiting for his blood work to come back to see the extensiveness of the carbon monoxide poisoning. It's important that he remains calm," Nurse Deidre said, giving Sierra a concerned glance. "So, whatever you were discussing before." She splayed cracked hands out in front of her. "And it's none of my business. You need to table it until we figure out what's going on with your husband."

Sierra pursed her lips, then looked down at Cedrick. "I'm staying." She retrieved her phone from the sink. "You're more important than this job."

"No," he yelled, sitting upright staring into her eyes. "Go to work."

Cedrick's blood pressure spiked on the heart monitor, and the beeping alerts increased.

"I need you to calm down, Mr. Dalton," the nurse said, then placed her focus on Sierra.

Sierra searched the pleading manner in Cedrick's dark eyes, then observed the monitor. "I think it's best that I go." She leaned in, planting a tender kiss on his tense lips. "I'll get back as soon as I can."

Chapter 7

As soon as Sierra and the nurse departed, Cedrick reached along the side of the bed and grabbed the clear plastic drawstring bag that housed his clothing. He rifled through his belongings until he found his phone. Pushing himself upward with his feet, Cedrick held the power button down until the white screen appeared.

The botched suicide attempt had perilous repercussions. Cedrick had to account for his actions, and he didn't know how he was going to explain to Sierra why he tried to take his life.

Several emails and text message notifications pinged right after Cedrick entered his passcode. The Smokehouse alerts were sounding off like fireworks on the Fourth of July. Cedrick always came in early to smoke the meat that had marinated overnight. He sent a text to his Sous Chef, handing him the reins for the next couple of days. He wasn't in any condition to deal with the restaurant business, and since the Sous Chef was second-in-command, he knew the Smokehouse was in more than capable hands.

Pressing the home button, Cedrick switched to check his email.

The suicide letter he wrote to Sierra glared back at him— unsent. A smidgen of the built-up tension released, causing his shoulders to slump, and the veins in his neck to soften. He'd explained way too much in that email— more than he was willing to discuss on this side of the grave. Cedrick tapped the cancel icon at the top of the screen, and the next email appeared, but not before the sound of an airplane taking off filtered through the room.

"No," he hollered. "What have I done?"

Staring at the phone in disbelief for several seconds, Cedrick let the phone slip from his hand. It fell in his lap with a dull thud.

He'd hit send by mistake. Now his suicide note and all the secrets he'd imparted in it was on its way to Sierra.

Cedrick's bottom lip dropped open, leaving his mouth drier than sawdust on a wooden floor. He closed his eyes tight, attempting to stave off the wretched thumping inside of his head. "Please forgive me," he cried, punching the mattress repeatedly with force.

The heart monitor sang a familiar tune.

With trembling hands, he picked up the phone and glared with pain in his heart at the empty Outbox folder. The suicide email he'd sent Sierra would reach her in moments.

"I've ruined everything."

"I thought I told you to relax," Nurse Deidre reprimanded in playful banter, rushing into the room with a woman in scrubs and one with a white lab coat in tow. "This is Dr. Simmons."

"What have I done?"

"Hi, Cedrick," Dr. Simmons said, moving in closer.

"What— have— I— done?" He snatched the blood pressure cuff off in one motion, swung his legs around, then stood.

"Whoa! Wait a minute," Nurse Deidre warned.

"I have to get to Sierra." Cedrick pulled his pants out of the bag.

"This isn't a good idea," Dr. Simmons cautioned, touching his arm.

He moved around her like she was a paper doll, losing his balance. The doctor and nurse braced Cedrick to keep him from falling.

He shrugged them off and staggered backward. "I have to go,"

Cedrick shouted.

"We could use some help in here," Nurse Deidre bellowed equally as loud.

Priscilla walked in, leaning on a four-prong metal cane. Her ash-brown hair caressed her jawline, framing her face. "What's going on in here?"

"Mom," Cedrick called out, still tussling with the doctor and nurse. "What are you—— they won't let me go."

"Ma'am," Dr. Simmons said, but Priscilla hushed her with the rise of her hand.

"Let him go. I got this," Priscilla ordered in a tone too mild for the situation.

"Ma'am——"

"He's not going anywhere," Priscilla reassured, gazing at Cedrick. "Release him."

Dr. Simmons glanced at Nurse Deidre, then nodded. They loosened their grips at the same time.

Cedrick stood there defeated, chest heaving harder than a toddler who couldn't have his way.

"Give me a moment alone with my son, please."

Though hesitant, they left the room.

"Mom. What are you doing here?" Cedrick asked, trying to catch his breath.

"You're not happy to see me?" she teased, patting the mattress.

Cedrick eased down, and Priscilla covered his legs with a thin white blanket before lowering herself into the chair next to his bed.

"Sierra called. She told me something I found very disturbing and hard to believe," Priscilla said in a concerned tone. She leveled a steady gaze on her son. "Is it true?"

Cedrick lowered his head.

"Why, son?" Priscilla lifted his chin. "After everything we've been through. After everything, you've overcome—— why now?" She gently squeezed his chin forcing him to lift his head and meet her gaze. "You have plenty to live for—— a beautiful wife, children who adore you, your dream career. You have much to be thankful for, son. Why risk throwing that away and exposing your family to such a loss?"

Silence hung in the air for a moment.

"Victoria's in town."

Priscilla's brown eyes grew wide with surprise. "The girl with the white patch of hair?"

"Yes."

She fell back in the seat. Her hand was coming up to rest over her heart. "Do you think it's a coincidence?"

"I don't know, and that's the problem," he whispered, pressing the button to adjust the bed to a more comfortable angle. He was silent for several seconds, a barrage of emotions scattering across his face. "Is there a statute of limitations on murder?"

"Self-defense," Priscilla corrected. She reached out and covered his hand with her own. She squeezed reassuringly. "I've told you that you no longer have to worry about that."

As much as Cedrick wanted to believe that, he couldn't. The day his father brutally attacked his mother changed his life forever. Priscilla made the mistake of answering the doorbell without wearing her hijab. She'd spoke with the mailman too long for his father's liking and no sooner than she closed the door, he accused her of disrespecting him and beat her face beyond recognition.

"But the cops may say it was murder since we ran," Cedrick countered.

"Killing yourself isn't the answer. Your kids need you, and so do I."

"But what about Sierra? Cedrick asked. "I'd sent her an email confessing to everything. She'll never understand—— her background's different. She'll never look at me the same." He twisted his wedding band. "I don't want my wife to be afraid of me."

"Again … self-defense. And if she's half the woman I've pegged her to be, she'll give you the benefit of the doubt." Priscilla paused, touching Cedrick's leg. "She's a mother … she'll understand. Trust in your wife, Cedrick. Trust in her love."

* * *

Sierra drove home, changed clothes, bandaged her injured feet, slipped on patent leather Mary Jane's, then rushed to the office building. She swapped the comfortable shoes for a pair of three-inch heels on the ride up to the twentieth floor. Flats were frowned upon in the workplace. She shot off the elevator moving as fast as she could. It was difficult at times because her feet throbbed in pain. The usual buzz around the office was subdued, a sure sign that company was on the floor.

She whizzed by her desk, eyeing the disarrayed papers and scowled.

"Where's Edward?" Sierra asked, Yvonne, Mark Smithe's assistant.

"In his office stewing," she warned, never shifting her focus from the computer. "He's been ringing your line every two minutes. Be careful, girl."

"Great," she mumbled, checking the time.

She had twenty minutes to spare, that was enough time to go over the documents for the meeting. Glancing at the disarray on her desk again, she fixed her face, then tapped on the door.

"Yes," Edward responded in an agitated tone.

She entered, masking the shock on her face at the equivalent mess on his desk.

Edward pushed upward with force, sending his chair rolling backward, crashing into the bookshelf. He took long strides around to the front of the desk. "You had me worried for a minute," he snapped, glancing at his watch. "But I knew you'd come through."

The sarcasm in Edward's tone made her blood boil. Sierra clipped the words that were about to roll off her tongue and apologized for the mix-up. She opened the file and went over the specifics, all the while disturbed by her bosses' lack of empathy.

"This is great," Edward commented, straightening his tie and fastening his suit jacket. "Take care of this mess."

"Would saying please and thank you be too much to ask for you asshole?" she mumbled after he left the office. Slipping off her heels and sitting in his chair, she tried to breathe through the pain. She was starting to regret not letting the paramedic see to her injured feet. At the very least she could have gotten something to relieve the pain.

Sierra called her husband as she arranged the files in alphabetical order, according to the client's last name and placed them in the file cabinet. Sierra felt like she was cleaning up after one of her children. Pushing that thought out of her mind, she tried to hurry through her task.

"Hey, honey. How are you feeling?" Sierra asked when she heard Cedrick's voice. She placed the scattered business cards in the cardholder.

"Still waiting on the test results," he replied in a sad tone. "I'm sorry, sweetheart."

"No—— I'm sorry for running out the way I did," she countered, lifting the two picture frames that were laid face down on the desk. "I shouldn't have left you like that, regardless of what you said. My job is never more important than you."

"You shouldn't have to risk losing your job because of something I did, Sierra."

"We'll discuss it later," she soothed. "Did mom make it?"

"You didn't have to call my mother."

"Someone needed to be there with you." She shook her head. "You shouldn't be there struggling with things alone."

She glanced at the photo of Edward and his wife, Jenesis, and wondered how she could love such a temperamental man. Placing the frame in its spot, Sierra grabbed the second photo, a wedding picture of Edward's son, Lennox and his wife, Victoria.

"Say what?" she mumbled under her breath, resting her elbows on the desk.

"Have you checked your emails today?" Cedrick inquired, his voice skittish.

Sierra glared at the beautiful woman in the sweetheart neckline wedding gown with the gorgeous patch of white hair swooped to one side—— the same as the woman's hair from the restaurant. She'd seen that photo a million times, but it never held her attention until today.

"Huh?"

"I sent you an email. If you haven't opened it yet, please delete it," Cedrick instructed.

Sierra couldn't tear her eyes away.

Edward talked emphatically against Lennox moving to his wife's hometown of Reno. He eventually accepted it, later praising his son for honoring her wishes no matter how much he was opposed. Edward hadn't mentioned Lennox being in town. Why was his wife here, and why was she talking to her husband? This was too close to be mere coincidence.

"What's the woman's name from the restaurant?"

Silence floated in the air.

"The fangirl," Sierra said between clenched teeth. She quickly pulled the phone away from her ear when the office door opened.

"Dad, it's me," a woman said happily peeking her head in Edward's office.

For a few uncomfortable seconds, both women were transfixed staring at each other.

"Never mind," Sierra spoke into the phone with slow deliberation before gingerly standing up. "She just walked in."

"Sier——"

She placed the handset back in its cradle ending the call.

"I'm looking for Edward Banks," the woman said. "He's expecting me."

Sierra glanced down at the picture. "And you are?" she asked, even though she knew the answer, sliding her feet into her heels and coming from behind the desk. Sierra embraced the pain. It kept her calm.

"Victoria Banks," she confirmed, stepping into the office. "Didn't I see you yesterday with Uwez—— Cedrick?"

"Yes. And how do you know my husband?" Sierra inquired, folding her arms and leaning her backside against the desk.

"We grew up together. We've been best friends since the fourth grade."

"You must take me as some kind of fool, Victoria," Sierra remarked, glaring at the beautiful bombshell. "You're not even from Chicago, so how did y'all grow up together?"

Victoria stepped closer. "You seem to know more about me than you let on."

Sierra grabbed the wedding photo from the desk. "You're Lennox's wife." She shoved the picture in her direction. "And you're from Reno, Nevada—— try again."

Victoria's expression was unreadable. "Kindly tell my father-in-law I'm here," she said, taking purposeful strides to the door. "I'll be in the lobby."

Chapter 8

Something was going on, and Sierra was determined to find out what. The same woman at the restaurant just strutted into her boss' office like she owned it.

Sierra's employer closed the deal with Eastside Development. Under normal circumstances, she would've been thrilled, but the outcome resulted in extra paperwork that had a swift deadline. The kind that consumed the entire day and squashed any opportunity Sierra would've had to speak with Victoria.

She wanted answers, but Sierra hadn't been able to reach Cedrick since they'd spoken earlier, and Priscilla's phone was going straight to voicemail. Her insides knotted with worry.

Five o'clock couldn't have come soon enough. Sierra slipped on her flats, signed out for the day and drove to the hospital. Crazy thoughts filtered her mind, but she forced herself to focus on Cedrick's well-being until he could tell her what was up with Victoria.

* * *

"I'm here to visit Cedrick Dalton," she said to the security person at the desk.

"What unit?"

"I'm not sure," she replied, dialing Priscilla's number for the umpteenth time. "He was in the ER this morning, but they said he'd been admitted and that I had to come to the main entrance."

"Last name, Dalton, right?" the security person repeated, typing the name into the computer. "He's on the ninth floor, ICU, room 903."

A sudden intake of air, dried her throat, leaving her tongue pasty. "Thanks," she mumbled, heading to the elevators, oblivious to the people and noises surrounding her.

Why didn't Priscilla call? She'd promised to keep her updated on Cedrick's condition. Worst case scenarios filled Sierra's thoughts, and she could only imagine how his mother might be feeling. Her only son tried to… Sierra shook her head and leaned against the railing inside the elevator. She couldn't allow herself to think about that.

Sierra stepped off the elevator on the ninth floor. Instant sadness washed over her as a flood of sobbing people spilled out of the family waiting area a few feet down from where she stood.

"Pardon me," she said with a gentle tone while maneuvering through the grieving crowd.

"I can't believe granny's gone," a woman cried, embracing an older gentleman with sparse gray hair.

"It was God's will, my darling," the man responded dabbing his eyes with a handkerchief. "My sweet lady will always live in my soul. She's resting with our heavenly father now and has eternal peace. I can't be sad about that."

Sierra tried not to make eye contact, but she couldn't help it. How could this man be so positive after losing someone he loved? Clearly, he understood the meaning of life in a way she didn't. Her husband attempted suicide. He chose to leave her and the girls behind. Sierra could never understand that.

"Sorry for your loss," Sierra said, offering a compassionate smile.

"Thank you," he replied, breaking the embrace with the young woman he'd been talking to, then placed a hand on Sierra's forearm. "My prayers are with you and whomever you're here to visit. Know that God is able." Then he stepped aside to let her pass.

"I appreciate your kind words."

Sierra walked to room 903 and froze in the doorway for a moment, then made a beeline to a sleeping Priscilla. "Why is he in that?" she asked, pointing to an oversized clear cylinder while tapping Priscilla on the shoulder.

"Hey, sweetie. It's not as bad as it looks," Priscilla explained, extending her arms above her head, yawning. "It's an oxygen chamber. His blood test showed that the carbon monoxide levels were higher than expected. Dr. Simmons said the chamber provides pressurized oxygen which will enhance the body's natural healing process much faster than the mask alone."

Sierra dropped her tote on the window ledge, then examined the contraption. "Can he hear me?" she asked, gazing at her husband lying on his back with his eyes closed.

"Sure, he can," Priscilla replied, leaning on her cane as she scooted to the edge of the reclining chair. "The doctor gave him a sedative. He's been a bit worked up."

Sierra placed her hand on the chamber; it was cool to the touch. She took a moment to gather herself. *This was just too much.*

"I'm sorry I didn't call you with an update, Sierra. I know this must be overwhelming for you."

"That's an understatement," Sierra choked out.

"Oh, honey. I feel horrible. I was planning to step out and call you to let you know how Cedrick was doing. The next thing I knew you were waking me up. Pull that chair over," Priscilla instructed. "He'll be sleeping for at least another hour. Sit down. Give yourself some time to relax."

That's what Sierra needed, to turn her brain off, but that was impossible. She drug the chair alongside her mother-in-law, then lifted her phone and laptop from her tote.

Priscilla placed her hand on Sierra's knee. "Contrary to what this looks like, Cedrick's a fighter. Don't you worry. He's going to bounce back from this."

"How do you know?"

"Because he's been through much worst," she replied.

"Like what?" Sierra asked, angling her body toward Priscilla.

A shadow crossed his mother's face. "Cedrick's a good man. He loves you and those girls with every fiber of his being," she stated, squeezing Sierra's knee. "Don't hold his past against him."

Sierra tilted her head to the side. "What does that mean? Why would I ever do that, Priscilla?"

When her mother-in-law hesitated, Sierra grew impatient. She stood up and began pacing.

"What is going on, Priscilla. I can feel it. There's something hovering over us right now that I can't see, but I know it's there. Cedrick wouldn't just up and try to commit suicide. He wouldn't just check out on the girls and me without cause. He's stronger than that," she said in a voice laced with anger. "We are stronger than that."

"He was protecting me," Priscilla blurted out.

Sierra stilled. "Who?"

"Cedrick. Haashim was an evil man, and an even worse husband and father."

"I thought Cedrick's father's name was Brian."

"It is, but his given name's Haashim," Priscilla responded, wringing her hands.

Sierra frowned, taking in the change in Priscilla's demeanor. "He's Muslim?"

"Yes," she said, gazing at Cedrick.

"Okay. So, what's the big deal?" Sierra replied, "I'm confused."

"I've said too much." Priscilla leaned forward on the cane and stood. "I'll be back."

"Wait," Sierra called after her mother-in-law, but she hurried out of the room. Sierra started to go after her, but something she couldn't name kept her rooted to her spot. Was it fear? First, Victoria showed up out the blue, then Cedrick tried to take his life, and now Priscilla's speaking in code. *What the hell's going on today?* Sierra wondered. She'd give Cedrick's mother some time, but she was determined to get to the bottom of all this. Tonight.

Needing a distraction, Sierra called her mother to give her an update and check on the girls.

"Mommy," Carrington squealed. "Where are you? How's daddy?"

"I'm at the hospital with daddy and——"

"Is he okay?"

Sierra glanced over at her husband, pursing her lips. "He's going to be just fine. The doctor wants to keep an eye on him, but I promise he's okay."

"Can I see him?" Carrington asked.

"Not today, but soon," she replied, firing up the laptop. "Where's your granny?"

"I'm right here, honey," Marva said. "Carrington, how do you take this phone off of hands-free?"

Sierra allowed herself the luxury of a chuckle. Carrington always had to show her granny how to operate her iPhone. Anything beyond making a phone call was foreign territory for her mother.

"How's Lena?"

"She's sleeping, finally." Marva exhaled, her voice filled with relief. "She knew granny needed a break and petered out twenty minutes ago. How's Cedrick?"

Sierra filled her mom in on everything that Priscilla told her, including the strange conversation, as she opened her personal email.

"*I love you. I'm sorry,*" Sierra said, reading the subject of an email she received from Cedrick early this morning.

"I love you, too, but what are you sorry about?" Marva questioned.

Sierra skimmed the text. Her heart plummeted faster than Number 45's approval rating.

"Mom—— Cedrick sent me..." Sierra's voice faltered, "A suicide email."

The silence on the other end of the phone matched the emptiness in Sierra's soul.

Priscilla entered the room with two brown Styrofoam cups with black lids. They exchanged a glance, and Sierra knew beyond any doubt, that the conversation they had ten minutes earlier, had everything to do with what she'd just read.

"Momma. I have to go."

"I can drop the girls off at Crystal's if you need me," Marva countered. "You shouldn't be alone right now."

"Thanks, but please don't bring auntie Crystal into this. I'll be fine," she sniffled. "Priscilla's back. I'll keep you posted. I love you."

Sierra ended the call and placed the phone face down in her lap.

Priscilla extended a cup to Sierra, but it hung in the midair. Instead, Sierra stared at her with an expectant look. With a deep, soul-wrenching sigh, she lowered the cup to the table and sat down across from Sierra. Folding her hands in her lap, she stared her daughter-in-law in the eyes. "Cedrick killed his father."

A loud gasp escaped Sierra's mouth.

A single tear trickled down Priscilla's face. "As I said earlier, Haashim was an evil man."

Sierra balked, walking toward the window, gazing at the panoramic view of Lake Michigan. "I wasn't expecting you to say that. I thought it was an accident. That maybe he fell and hit his head, or something and Cedrick didn't do anything to help him."

Priscilla hobbled over to the window. "He who is without sin cast the first stone."

"Don't spout bible verses at me," Sierra warned. "Thou shall not kill."

Anger spurred Priscilla into action. She stood up to her full height, her cane forgotten. "Don't you dare judge me...or my son. Haashim was an abusive man who beat Cedrick daily," she spat through clenched teeth with knitted brows. "He was an extremist when it came to Islam. Cedrick never had the kind of childhood that Carrington and Lena have. Can you imagine what that's like? How hard it was on both of us to walk on eggshells day after day? Not knowing what would set my husband off, or throw him into a rage?"

Sierra remained silent. Tears flowed haphazardly down her cheeks. Numb, she turned and blankly stared out the window. At that moment, she realized that she didn't know her husband at all. His past and what he'd been through in his childhood. "Why didn't he tell me?"

Priscilla slowly crossed the room. She placed her hand on Sierra's shoulder. "He wanted to protect you, Carrington and Lena from his past—from his pain. Cedrick couldn't ask questions or make demands. He was seven years old the first time Hasshim hit him with a closed fist—— all because he asked why he prayed to Allah instead of Jesus like his friends?" Priscilla frowned. "He was seeking understanding. It didn't warrant a thrashing." Priscilla's voice cracked with the remembered pain. "Cedrick couldn't even leave the dinner table to go to the bathroom, without getting backhanded. And if he wet himself, he got it ten times worse."

Sierra's entire body trembled. She couldn't imagine anyone putting their hands on her girls, not even their father.

"Visualize someone beating Carrington, for being the person she is," Priscilla pressed, now needing the support of her cane. "She's so much like her daddy was as a kid. Inquisitive, adventurous, silly, smart. Can you imagine someone trying to squelch that?"

Remorse overcame Sierra as she turned to face Priscilla with tears in her eyes, her chest constricting with pain at her snap to judgment.

"Imagine that person was her father and you were powerless to stop it?" Priscilla's chest heaved as pools of tears escaped their home and flowed down her cheeks. "That man deserved what he got," she cried. "And I for one am glad the bastard is gone."

Chapter 9

"Are you ready to talk to me?" Cedrick asked Sierra, grabbing the remote from the nightstand and placing the TV on mute. "I've been home for five days now. Thanksgiving's next week. We can't continue like this."

"I want things the way they used to be, but that isn't an option," Sierra replied, sliding under the covers.

"I've played this scenario over in my head a million times, and the outcome has always been *this*. It's what kept me silent when I needed to level with you."

Sierra gazed at him. "What do you mean?"

"You looking at me differently," he countered, scooting closer and wrapping an arm around her to pull her close. "I love you. I was scared of losing you. I'm *still* scared of losing you."

"But you were going to leave me with two kids to raise alone ..."

Cedrick glanced off into the distant corner of the bedroom; his eyes fixated on a wall portrait of the girls in pastel purple dresses, each girl holding a sunflower.

"Why couldn't you trust me with the truth?" Sierra asked, propping herself up on her elbow.

"Because I was afraid of the police or FBI finding me or interrogating you," Cedrick confessed. "You can't tell them what you don't know." He ran his hand along the side of her face. "I was protecting you and the kids."

Sierra kissed the tip of his nose. "Cedrick, *we* are a team," she stressed. "What affects you, affects me— affects our family. I feel bad for misjudging things when your mom told me about your past. Honestly, I couldn't understand until your mother made me see things from both your sides. When she asked how I'd have felt if it was Carrington, I realized I couldn't judge you because I wasn't in your shoes. And for that I'm sorry."

Cedrick hugged her tight and kissed the top of her head. "Sweetheart, there's nothing to apologize for. I should've told you. My only defense was that I was scared to death and I'm more frightened now than before." He rolled onto his back taking her with him.

"But why?"

"What if they come for me and say you've been hiding a fugitive all these years and you get locked up? I'd rather kill myself before I let that happen. I don't care what happens to me, but what about you, and our girls? I couldn't risk the authorities or the press hounding my family for something I did."

Sierra climbed out of bed and walked around to his side. "C'mon," she said, reaching for Cedrick's hand.

He pulled on a pair of gray sweatpants that laid at the foot of the bed, then grabbed her hand. Sierra walked him down the hall to Carrington's room.

"Your twin in there." Sierra opened the door and pointed to their daughter. "Needs you. If it weren't for Carrington, you wouldn't be alive," she stammered. "God didn't give you another chance for you to second guess being here."

Cedrick rested his head along the doorframe, watching his first-born sleep peacefully. Carrington Dalton was proof that he got it right. She loved him the way Cedrick loved his father. The difference is that Cedrick returned her love and affection tenfold. His father never had.

Sierra tugged his arm, pulling Cedrick from his thoughts as they walked across the hall to Lena's room. "This one loves you more than she loves me." Sierra snickered. "Da-Da-Da-Da-Da, is all I hear."

Cedrick laughed. "That's my girl; that's why."

"Whatever." Sierra nudged him. She took both his hands securely in her own. Only when he made eye contact did she continue. "Remember that when you feel like there's no way out. They need you, and so do I. We are a family. That will never change, Cedrick. Never."

He wrapped his arms around his wife, and she buried her head in his chest.

"I love you." Cedrick pulled Sierra into a tight embrace, stroking the back of her curly fro. "Thanks for reminding me what's important."

"No matter what happens, we face it together," she stated. "Never forget that."

"I won't," he assured her.

"So, tell me all about Victoria."

"Vicki saved my life a million times over," he admitted, locking his fingers in Sierra's and walking to their bedroom. He closed the door behind them. "She was the only person other than my mom who knew my dad beat me." Cedrick lowered onto the bed and turned his back toward his wife. "It's harder to talk about than I thought."

"You don't have to be ashamed," she reassured Cedrick, laying her cheek against his back. "I'd never judge you or make you feel small, and I'll always protect your secrets," Sierra said, maneuvering to Cedrick's side and stroking his face. "I love you."

He turned toward Sierra and kissed the back of her hand. "I love you more," he replied, laying on his back and pulling her down with him. Sierra snuggled in Cedrick's arms and laid her head on his chest. Wrapping his arm around her back, he held her close. "My dad … he enjoyed hurting me. I don't know why and unfortunately, I'll never know. I was a kid. How could my own father hate me so much?"

"That was more about him than you and whatever issues he had within."

"My brain knows that it wasn't my fault, but the little boy inside who was terrified of his father still has questions," Cedrick said with a deep sigh. "This is where Vicki comes in. I had no friends until her family moved next door when I was seven. She brought me out of my shell and didn't even know it." A small chuckle escaped his mouth. "I used to watch her play on the front lawn from my living room window all the time."

"Stalker-ish," Sierra teased, poking Cedrick in the side.

"Whatever." He laughed, pushing her finger away. "Every time Vicki glanced my way I would duck down, hoping she hadn't seen me. I was afraid she could tell what my father did to me just by looking at me. Then one day, Vicki rang my doorbell and asked my mother if I could come out and play. I was so scared, but my mom encouraged me to make a new friend. I thought my dad would see me having fun and hit me because of it. I swear the sound of my laughter set him off. Anyway, that was the beginning of our friendship."

"Victoria's been a part of your life for a long time," Sierra commented, "How long before you told her about the abuse?"

"Two years. Vicki hugged me, and her exact comment was, *that's why you look sad all the time, but everything's going to be okay because I'm your friend now*. I made her promise not to tell anyone, not even her parents. She promised she wouldn't."

"Sounds like Victoria was loyal and trustworthy.

"She was." Cedrick paused for a moment. "I was envious of Vicki's relationship with her dad. You could tell he truly loved her just by the way he talked to her. There was a tenderness to his masculine voice that always shown through his tough exterior. He'd take her bike riding and would sometimes play tea party with Vicki and her dolls when she had no one to play with. Her dad would always open the door for her whenever they got in the car. My dad never did that for my mom, and she was his wife."

"He sounds like an amazing man and father," Sierra commented, leaning into Cedrick. "Just like you."

"Thanks, sweetheart. But you're biased."

"That doesn't make it any less true and the fact that you *are,* without having that example from your father, is even more amazing," Sierra said, hugging Cedrick tightly. "You are everything to me. To this family. Don't ever forget that."

* * *

The following morning, Cedrick rose early and prepared breakfast for the family. He took the conversation he and Sierra had to heart and restructured his schedule, so he could be there for the ones he loved the most. Whatever the outcome, Cedrick would deal with the fall out when it came.

"Ooooo, Mommy. You cooked bacon," Carrington shouted, rounding the corner into the kitchen. "It smells soooo—— Daddy," she screamed with delight and launched herself into his arms. "You don't have to work today?"

"I go back tomorrow."

Carrington's face lit up brighter than the lights on a Christmas tree. "So, you'll be here when I get home from school?"

"That's the plan." Cedrick winked, handing Carrington a plate filled with bacon, eggs, raisin toast, and sliced kiwi.

"I thought I was dreaming," Sierra said with her nose stuck in the air. "But nope, that *is* bacon I smell." She sauntered over in an open robe, wearing a bra and pajama pants, plucking a juicy brown strip from an aluminum pie pan lined with a napkin. "And my husband home for breakfast."

"Good morning." Cedrick smiled as his lips met hers. "Juan's opening up today. He's been doing a pretty good job of running things in my absence," he acknowledged, handing Sierra a plate filled with all the trimmings.

"Thanks, babe," she said sauntering to the table taking a seat beside Carrington. "Oooooo. What's this? Sierra lowered onto the chair, then removed a folded card with her name on the front, and a single long stem rose from the placemat.

Carrington grinned, then glanced at her daddy. He winked as he waited for Sierra to read the card.

Several seconds passed before Sierra glanced upward in that way that made his nature rise. The expected result of desire brimming in his loins was instantaneous.

Cedrick walked over to Carrington and placed his hands over her ears. "Don't start something we don't have time to finish," he warned in a low, deep voice.

She beamed with pleasure. "Thank you." Sierra lifted the flower to her nose and inhaled.

"You're welcome." Cedrick smiled, keeping his focus on Sierra's mesmerizing eyes. "I'll take care of the girls this morning. You relax and enjoy your breakfast."

* * *

Cedrick dropped the girls off at school and daycare, then headed home, but not before placing a call to Chef Brasseur in hopes of catching him before the restaurant opened.

"Hello. Is Chef Brasseur available?"

"I'm sorry, Sir, but we're closed. You can try him after eleven," the polite woman on the other end of the phone informed Cedrick.

"Tell Gabriel it's Cedrick Dalton on the line. If he wishes for me to call back during regular business hours, I will. But could you please relay that message. I'll hold. Thank you."

If Cedrick knew anything, he was confident Chef Brasseur was at the restaurant early, overseeing things. That's how he did it at The Smokehouse.

A few minutes passed, then Chef Brasseur bellowed into the phone. "Hey, Cedrick. What can I do you for?"

"About twenty minutes of your time, if you can spare them," Cedrick shot back.

"Where and when?"

Chef Brasseur agreed, and they met at the coffee shop around the corner from the restaurant. Cedrick presented the chef with an offer he hoped he couldn't refuse.

"It's been rumored that your restaurant's slated to close by the end of next year," Cedrick mentioned with a gloomy sigh. "I'm sorry these new tax tariffs recently implemented have affected your business."

"Had I known it was going to be like this, I would've held off on the remodel. Now, I'm barely hanging on," Chef Brasseur said; his French accent dull and dry. "I've been in business for over ten years. I didn't struggle this much when I first started. The overhead's killing me. I don't know how I'm going to tell my employees."

"What do you think about partnering with me at The Smokehouse, offering French barbecue?" Cedrick asked, enthusiasm dripping from his tongue. "Our customers can have the best of both worlds. Your balsamic chicken and fig brochettes and marinated monkfish are grilled delicacies that I enjoy, along with half of Chicago according to the reviews on The Infatuation." Cedrick smiled. "I'll have room for you, your Sous Chef, and a few staff members. This way, you can still cook the food you love, pay off your debts, and keep most of your clientele."

"Sounds intriguing." Chef Brasseur hummed, sipping his hot chocolate. "Let me discuss it with my partner, and I'll get back to you."

* * *

Cedrick drove home with a peace that had always eluded him. Helping a fellow entrepreneur filled him with pleasure. He could've been in Chef Brasseur's situation, but that was only part of the reason for the joy in his heart.

The past didn't haunt him with the same intensity as before. He had Sierra to thank for that. She discharged his worst fear, at least one of them. She didn't pack the kids and flee when his ugly truth fell in her lap, considering the way it was exposed, would've given the most dedicated person pause.

Cedrick went downstairs into his home gym in the basement and did cardio combined with weights for an hour then hopped in the shower. He opened his mouth, allowing the water pellets to dance on the back of his throat until his mouth was full, then he'd shoot them out between his teeth like a fountain.

Long showers were forbidden as a child. Five minutes max, just enough time to wash and rinse, and Cedrick could forget about shampooing his thick locs. Shaving them gave Cedrick great pleasure when they moved to Chicago.

As an adult, his shower routine was pretty much the same. Cedrick didn't have time to indulge, but today, he did. Thirty minutes in, he was like Fred Astaire singing in a monsoon and enjoying every minute until the doorbell rang.

Patting himself dry, Cedrick wrapped a robe around his damp body and rushed to the front door. He opened it without checking the peephole.

"Well ..." Victoria blushed, grinning at him as if she'd won the lottery.

Cedrick stared dumbfounded.

"You going to let me in or what? I wouldn't want all of that to catch a cold." She gestured, waving her hand from his chest to midsection.

He stepped aside so she could enter, tugging his robe as Mr. Alexander, the neighborhood dog sitter, walked by with his canine friends.

"Good day, Cedrick," the older man greeted with a nod and a suspicious gaze. "How's the misses?"

"She's fine. I'll tell Sierra you asked about her."

Cedrick closed the door and faced Victoria. "How'd you know where I live?"

"Since you wouldn't return any of my phone calls, I had to get creative."

"I guess a straight answer is too much to ask for?" Cedrick smirked, shaking his head. "Some things never change."

Victoria slid her coat off and laid it across the back of the charcoal leather sofa. "I asked my father-in-law for Sierra's address."

"And he gave it to you. No questions asked."

"I *said* I had to get creative," she replied, parking her behind on the sofa, angling her weight to one side.

Cedrick excused himself and got dressed. When he returned, Victoria had poured herself a glass of orange juice and reclaimed her seat on the sofa.

"Why doesn't your wife know about me or our friendship?" Victoria asked, glancing upward at Cedrick. "Lennox knows all about you."

He rubbed his temple, perplexed that Victoria went to such lengths to find out where he lived to ask him why he didn't talk about her to his wife. It didn't make sense. Why was that so important?

"Lennox knows you were my best friend growing up," she clarified. "Sierra doesn't know you lived in Reno according to our short conversation. Why wouldn't you tell her about me? I share all the important aspects of my life with my husband."

"She knows about you," Cedrick said, sitting next to Victoria.

"Yeah … now she does."

"Vicki. There were things about my past that I don't ever want to speak on. Let alone share with anyone else——"

"That's how you feel?" She shot up, slamming the glass on the coaster so hard that the stem broke. "I'm a "thing" from your past that you'd rather forget. That's how you see me?" she snarled, snatching her coat.

"Wait," Cedrick hollered, reaching for her. "That's not what I meant."

Victoria opened the front door, but Cedrick pushed it closed. "Why are you so angry?"

She turned to face him, her eyes glazed over. Victoria gripped his t-shirt in her fist, pulling him down to her, planting a wet kiss on his lips. "When Uwezo Omari returns, let me know, 'cause I don't recognize this Cedrick person. Goodbye."

Chapter 10

Cedrick stared at the front door as though he expected it to talk suddenly. What just happened? What made Victoria so angry in a matter of seconds? He backtracked the conversation and couldn't think of anything that he said that would've warranted that hostility.

What Cedrick did know for certain, was what a goodbye-I'm-never-going-to-see-you-again kiss felt like. He wrote the rulebook on that one. Though Victoria never coming around again was for the best, Cedrick felt a loss, and he wondered if this was how she felt when he left all those years ago.

The faint sound of a ringing phone snapped Cedrick out of his trance. He jogged up the stairs, taking two at a time. Sierra's name flashed across the front of the screen, but the ringing ended by the time he pressed the button to answer. Six missed calls from her guaranteed an interrogation. Before he could call Sierra back, she'd called for the seventh time.

"What's going on? Is Victoria there?" Sierra inquired, her voice quivering. "Mr. Alexander said a woman he'd never seen before had entered my house."

"Really." Cedrick snorted, outdone by the audacity of his nosey neighbor.

Mr. Alexander never minded his own business. It's a good thing Cedrick didn't have anything to hide. Or did he?

"I don't have much time to talk before Yvonne comes back to her desk," Sierra mumbled in a hushed voice. "Yvonne told me Victoria had asked her for my address, then got huffy when she refused to give it to her. Then she overheard Wilkerson's assistant, give her my information." Sierra sighed into the phone. "It's taking every restraint I have not to confront her."

"Don't," Cedrick warned, squinting in the bathroom mirror, rubbing the colorful sticky substance from his lips. "It'll stir things up between you and Yvonne."

"True, but she needs to be reported," Sierra countered. "How many times has she given out employees or a client's personal information before?"

"I don't know, but to answer your first question," Cedrick began, stretching his lips, checking the corners of his mouth to make sure all the evidence of Victoria's lipstick had been wiped away. "Victoria did stop by."

"What did she want?"

"Long story short, to know why I didn't tell you about her," he said, washing his hands. "The conversation didn't go well. She misinterpreted what I was trying to say and stormed out."

Cedrick wasn't sure if he should tell Sierra about the kiss.

"You need to call her and see what she knows."

"What?"

"Just to be on the safe side," Sierra emphasized with a questioning tone. "I know she was here on business, but make sure that's all she was here for, you feel me?"

"I'd rather not."

"You said she was your best friend and helped you during that time, correct?" Sierra countered, but not waiting for a response. "You need to call her back. Do it now."

Cedrick gnawed his inner jaw until he pierced the flesh. "Babe, I really don't want to do this. I don't know what Victoria's true intentions are. In all the years you've worked for Edward, she's never been a part of anything going on at the firm. But now, all of a sudden around the anniversary of my dad's——" Cedrick paused to gather himself. The veins in his neck pulsated and pain shot upward causing the back of his head to hurt. "She shows up."

"That's why you need to——"

"And Mitch is a cop?"

"Who's Mitch?"

"Victoria's dad," Cedrick replied, walking over to the coffee table and picking up the broken pieces of glass.

Each piece represented the unknown factors in his life: uncertainty, his future, his freedom. The only thing Cedrick was sure of was his love for Sierra.

After a moment's pause, Sierra responded, "No worries. I'll see you when I get home. Yvonne's back."

* * *

Sierra hung up the phone just as Yvonne walked the short distance to her desk and fired up the computer. "Thanks for looking out."

"No problem, girlfriend. Obviously, Victoria didn't know we were friends. I don't know her and don't care who she is," Yvonne said, twisting an ink pen between her fingers. "I wasn't telling her anything."

Sierra smiled, appreciating her coworker and friend's loyalty as her fingers glided across the keyboard. She pulled the Eastside Development document up on the screen and scanned the contacts on the account.

"I'll show Victoria Banks how it's done," Sierra mumbled to herself, jotting down her phone number.

She'd take care of things. The apprehensiveness in Cedrick's voice was hard to miss, and she should've known better. It was too soon to ask that of him. Although he seemed okay on the outside, she knew he was still healing. He'd carried that burden by himself long enough. Now, it was Sierra's turn to protect their family.

She pressed the button for the elevator with car keys and lunch sack in hand. Complete privacy didn't exist in the office, except for the attorney's suite and she didn't have a legitimate reason to be in there.

Sierra entered the parking garage, thankful that the car was parked near the outer wall so that she could get a cell signal. She slid in the passenger's seat and emptied the contents of her lunch sack on the opposite seat.

After starting the car, the phone automatically switched to Bluetooth, connecting her cell to the interior speakers. She punched in Victoria's number and released a breath she wasn't aware she'd been holding. Not sure of what to expect once Victoria answered gave her anxiety, leaving her apprehensive like Cedrick. What would happen if she knew the truth?

"Hello. Who's this?" Victoria answered, sounding less than friendly.

For Victoria to be a professional woman, her gruff greeting startled Sierra.

"Sierra Dalton. Cedrick's wife."

"Hey." Victoria hesitated. "This is unexpected. Cedrick must've given you my number."

"No," Sierra responded, unfastening a Ziploc bag.

"Then how did——"

"The same way you obtained my address," Sierra shot back in a less than favorable tone, popping a grape in her mouth.

Sierra made sure Victoria understood that she knew what she did.

Also, that her husband didn't keep any secrets from her, they were on one accord.

"Kind of sucks, doesn't it?" Sierra commented, not looking for a response, but rather to put something on Victoria's mind. "What was so important for you to make an unannounced house call?"

"I …"

"Is there something you had to tell him? Or was there anything you needed to know, besides Cedrick not talking to me about you?" Sierra turned up a bottle of water, waiting for her response.

"I don't wanna come off as some crazy chick from his past. It's nothing like that," Victoria implored. "Cedrick's still my best friend, even though we haven't talked in years. I didn't know if he was dead, in jail, or what. He just disappeared from …"

"Reno." Sierra completed Victoria's sentence.

"Yeah," she replied, clearing her throat. "When I bumped into you at Edward's office, I got the impression you didn't know he was from Reno."

Victoria's observance was spot on, but Sierra wasn't going to confirm anything.

"Your presence caught me off guard," Sierra said, screwing the top on the empty water bottle. "I knew Edward's daughter-in-law's name was Victoria. I didn't know Cedrick's friend, Victoria *Weiss* and Lennox's wife, Victoria *Banks*, were one and the same. I'd never met anyone from Cedrick's hometown, besides his mother. I didn't have anyone to compare you to, except at the restaurant. Why'd you lie about knowing Cedrick?"

"… he asked me to."

Sierra opened her mouth to object but clamped down. Cedrick was so quick to get out of Chef Brasseur's restaurant that afternoon—— she believed Victoria.

"My only agenda is to reconnect with an old friend. If I were in your——" Victoria paused. "Let's say; I can understand your guard being up. A woman you've never met before, falling into your husband's life. It seems suspect."

"Very much so," Sierra admitted relaxing a bit.

They talked for another ten minutes. Sierra found Victoria to be harmless and amusing. In Sierra's gut, she believed this woman meant Cedrick nor her family any harm, so she extended an olive branch in hopes to ease Cedrick's mind.

"Thanksgiving's next week. If you're still in town, you and Lennox should join us for dinner. Cedrick smokes a turkey that'll make you slap your momma; it's so delicious and juicy."

"Oooo, how could I turn down that invite? Sounds scrumptious," Victoria said in an airy voice. "I'll most likely be flying solo, pun intended." She giggled. "Lennox is a pilot with Southwest Airlines. He never has Thanksgiving off."

"Then it's a go. I'll let you know what time dinner will be served."

Sierra ended the call, gathered her things, then headed back inside. She prided herself on being a good judge of character. She hoped this wasn't the one time her senses failed her.

Chapter 11

"I still can't believe she invited Victoria," Cedrick said to his mother as he set an extra place setting at the dining room table.

"Well, I'm excited to see her," Priscilla said, bouncing Lena on her lap. "I've always been curious to see what she'd become. That little girl ran around with you boys, with building blocks stuffed in her pockets and a roll of paper towels under her arm."

"I remember that." Cedrick chuckled, squeezing Lena's chubby cheeks. "Victoria drew blueprints of all the homes on the block on that roll of paper towels, then laminated them. She swore she'd be an architect someday."

"She's a darn good one, too from the looks of the Eastside Project design," Sierra chimed in, walking into the dining room with Carrington on her heels, carrying a festive centerpiece.

Cedrick glanced at Sierra and shook his head. She returned his pointed gaze.

"It's a shame Marva isn't going to be with us this Thanksgiving," Priscilla mentioned, breaking the unspoken tension.

"I'm missing my mom already," Sierra said, putting her focus on the harvest colored floral arrangement. "But if I'd won a free trip to the Caribbean, I'd be sipping a Piña Colada in a string bikini, saying happy Thanksgiving while digging my feet in the white sand too."

"Granny should've taken me with her," Carrington beamed, smacking her lips. "I could fit in her suitcase. Nobody would *even* know I was there."

"You're trying to get your granny locked up?" Cedrick teased. "She can't be smuggling kids out of the country."

"She might get away with getting her out the country," Sierra added, stepping back, gazing at the centerpiece. "But she will catch H. E. L. L. trying to get her back in. You know U. S. customs and border protection is a trip. Remember when they pulled me out of line at the airport on our way back from Nassau? They quadruple checked my passport and luggage and patted me down like a criminal."

"How could I forget our honeymoon." Cedrick grinned. "We'd been married all of seventy-two hours, and I was about to lose my wife over a piece of fruit."

Everyone burst out in hearty laughter.

"Heyyyy." Sierra shrugged. "I didn't know you couldn't bring fresh fruits and veggies into the states."

"Mom, you're funny," Carrington teased. "I learned about that in my social science class. Plant pests and diseases can be in the fruit and cause an outbreak like it did in the 1980s. All it takes is one piece of infected fruit, Mommy."

"Well," Sierra smirked, reaching over the table to shift the centerpiece more to the left so it'll be perfect. "I'll remember that next time."

"And Mommy, you didn't have to spell out hell, it's not a bad word. It's in the bible."

Sierra placed a hand on the back of the chair, then pointed to Cedrick. "You better get your daughter before we have one less thing to be thankful for."

"Watch it, Carrington." He whacked her upper arm with a cloth napkin. "Technic——"

The doorbell rang, rendering Cedrick silent.

"I'll get it." Carrington turned to bolt toward the front room, but Cedrick grabbed her arm.

"I got it," he glanced at Sierra, and she followed him to the front door. "I pray you know what you're doing."

Sierra slid her hand in his and squeezed. "There's only one way to find out," she remarked, reaching for the knob.

"Hey." Victoria waved. "I hope it's okay that I brought a plus one."

Cedrick glared at the man who was more of a father to him than his dad ever was. Though salt and pepper, Mitch Weiss looked the same. Broad shoulders that commanded attention through his tweed coat, strong jawline, and understanding mocha eyes that pierced your soul.

"Of course," Sierra replied, nudging Cedrick.

"Hi, Mr. Weiss," Cedrick extended his hand. "It's so good to see you."

Mitch shook his hand, then pulled him into an embrace, placing a kiss on Cedrick's cheek. "How're you doing, son?"

"Good. Please, come in." Cedrick stepped aside, thankful for the physical contact because the first thing he saw was a cop from his hometown. The embrace reminded Cedrick of the Mitch he knew as a kid. A caring and outspoken man who took time with the neighborhood kids to keep them on the right track. Mitch took them camping, to baseball games, and fishing at Pyramid Lake. Those outings were the childhood memories he cherished.

"I couldn't leave my dad by himself for the holiday. I hope this doesn't cause any problems," Cedrick overheard Victoria whisper to Sierra.

"None at all," Sierra replied. "I'll have Carrington set an extra place at the table."

"Pardon my manners," Victoria apologized. "This is Cedrick's wife, Sierra and this is my dad, Mitch."

"Nice to meet you." Sierra extended her hand, but Mitch pulled her into a light embrace.

"Likewise," he said with a warm smile.

Priscilla walked into the front room using a cane for support as Lena crawled close behind. "Mitchell Weiss," she said, annunciating every syllable of his name. "I'd know that voice anywhere."

With a huge grin, Mitch released Sierra and walked over to Priscilla. She dropped her cane and wrapped both arms around him. "It's been too long," Mitch said in a voice soft with affection, kissing Priscilla on the cheek, his lips lingering long enough to make Cedrick, Sierra, and Victoria glance at one another with a curious smirk.

Cedrick sidled up to Victoria and asked, "Did we miss something?"

"You tell me," she whispered.

All this time, Cedrick had been concerned with Mitch being the police. Him figuring out what happened and taking him to jail. Maybe Cedrick should've been asking why his mother wasn't concerned about Mitch finding out. What had been going on between them? When did it start, and did his father know? How did it continue? Mitch hadn't been around after they left Reno. Or had he?

"Daddy. Who are these people?" Carrington asked, entering the living room?

Cedrick squatted, picking up Priscilla's cane, then draped an arm across his daughter's shoulder. "This is my childhood friend Ms. Victoria and her dad, Mr. Weiss."

"Nice to meet you," Victoria said, extending her arms to hug Carrington, but she stayed at her dad's side.

"Hello, Ms. Victoria," Carrington said with a small wave.

Cedrick glanced down at Carrington. "You're not going to give her a hug?"

"No," she responded, her voice firm, but not disrespectful.

Cedrick's eyes shot over to Sierra who had been watching the interaction. She shrugged, bending to scoop up Lena.

"It's okay," Victoria remarked, giving Carrington her attention. "I don't hug strangers either, but by the end of the night, I won't be."

Everyone washed their hands and took a seat around the dining room table. Cedrick blessed the food, then carved the turkey.

"Is this the legendary smoked turkey Sierra told me about?" Victoria asked, putting collard greens on her plate.

Cedrick chuckled. "Sure is," he replied, cutting several slices before placing the tray on the table.

"Thanks for having us." Mitch smiled at Priscilla. "This is the first-family style Thanksgiving I've had since Doris died."

Victoria rubbed her dad's back. "I miss mom, too."

"I didn't know your mom passed. Sorry for your loss," Cedrick said, glancing at Victoria.

"It'll be four years on December first," Victoria recalled, leaning her head against Mitch's shoulder. "Thanksgiving and Christmas haven't been the same since." She put her focus on Carrington and Lena. "Enjoy your momma. Treat her right, always. You only get one."

Sierra and Victoria shared a compassion filled smile.

"What about daddies?" Carrington asked, stuffing a devil egg in her mouth. "They're special too."

"They most certainly are," Sierra added, leaning over, pecking Cedrick on the lips. "You girls struck gold when God chose this man to be your father."

Cedrick winked at Carrington, and she giggled.

"Do you miss your daddy?" Carrington asked Cedrick, wiping the crumbs from her mouth with a napkin. "You never talk about him."

Cedrick glanced at Sierra with alarm. This was not the conversation he wanted to have, especially not now.

"My dad died when I was a teenager——"

"I didn't know that." Victoria gasped, dropping her fork in the plate.

Mitch faced Priscilla, his eyes the size of tambourines. He opened his mouth to speak, but Priscilla slightly shook her head. Had Cedrick not been paying attention, he would've missed the movement.

"Was he sick like Papa Lou?" Carrington asked, staring at her daddy.

Cedrick didn't know how to answer his daughter's question. She'd never asked about her grandfather. Sierra's dad was larger than life up until the day he died from a ruptured brain aneurysm. Papa Lou loved those girls just as much as he did.

"Let's talk about something else," Sierra suggested, offering Carrington another serving of cranberry sauce. "It's okay to remember those who've gone before us, but let's be thankful for the family that's still here."

"Priscilla," Mitch said, touching her hand with an unreadable expression. "Does——"

"And let's be thankful for old friends." Priscilla smiled at Mitch, placing her other hand on top of his and squeezed.

"I couldn't agree more," Cedrick commented, swallowing the oversized lump in the middle of his throat.

After dinner, everyone gathered in the family room to enjoy eggnog, listen to music, and play scrabble. The crackling wood in the fireplace gave off a warmth that put Cedrick at ease.

Sierra laid Lena down, then joined everyone. "Are y'all ready for this butt whipping? The champ isn't here, and I'm the next best player."

"The Champ?" Victoria echoed, tucking several strands of hair behind her ear.

"Sierra's mother," Cedrick answered. "She massacres us every time." He glanced over his shoulder. "Mom, are you and Mitch going to play? I can sit this one out."

"We'll pass," Priscilla responded, sitting on a cozy sectional in the corner, conversing with Mitch.

Cedrick, Sierra, and Victoria shared a glance like the one they had when Mitch and Victoria arrived.

Midway through the game, Carrington asked if she could be excused. Her best friend, Brittney wanted to video chat with her on FaceTime. Cedrick gave her permission. As a result, the game moved a little faster, but he could barely keep up for staring at his mom and

Mitch while eavesdropping on their conversation.

"I did what you wanted," Mitch said, sipping his eggnog. "Although I hated every minute of it."

"You staying away wasn't what I wanted, but it was for the best," Priscilla countered.

"How can that be?" Mitch asked. "I've been miserable all these years. I lost my longtime friend." He leaned in closer to Priscilla. "I know I wanted more than you were willing or able to give at the time. I've always put your needs first. We aren't getting any younger, and nothing is keeping us from pursuing a loving relationship now," he said reaching for Priscilla's hand, but she pulled away.

Cedrick's eyelids narrowed at that gesture.

"Hey," Sierra said nudging his arm. "It's your turn."

"I'll pass," Cedrick replied with the wave of the hand, never taking his focus from his mom and Mitch.

"I don't think that's a good idea," Priscilla said with a frown. "It would make things too complicated, Mitch. Especially, considering Haashim."

What seemed like two friends catching up on old times quickly turned into a serious discussion. Their expressions were questioning, and their voices dropped to a whisper. Cedrick could no longer hear what was being said.

"Excuse me," Cedrick uttered, getting to his feet, approaching Priscilla and Mitch. He didn't like what he'd been seeing and now, his mom seemed upset. "Mom, is everything alright?"

"Yes, son," she replied, patting his hand with a smile that didn't quite reach her eyes.

"Are you sure?" he asked, with his full attention on Mitch.

"I'm sure."

Cedrick bent down and kissed her on the forehead. "Let me know when you're ready to go. It's too late for you to drive home by yourself."

"I'd already considered that," Priscilla commented. "I asked Mitch if he and Victoria could take me home, and he said yes."

"Oh, okay." Cedrick sauntered back over to the scrabble game.

Two hours later, everyone said their goodbyes.

"Crisis averted," Sierra whispered, slipping her arm around Cedrick's waist, waving as the car pulled off. "Mitch nor Victoria are a threat to our family. They seemed genuine. If not, they both need to win an Oscar for best performance."

"Maybe." He frowned, shutting the door. "Did you catch that weird vibe between my mom and Mitch?"

"What do you think it is?" Sierra asked.

"I don't know. Something's up," Cedrick mumbled, straightening the family room.

"You should sleep better tonight, knowing they aren't aware of the situation with your father," Sierra concluded, taking the empty glasses into the kitchen. "Did you see the look on Victoria's face? She couldn't fake that shock if she tried."

"You're right about that, but my mom and Mitch …"

"Yeah, I saw how chummy they were. Maybe there's some history between them that you don't know about."

"It's definitely something." Cedrick scowled, taking the glasses from Sierra and placing them in the dishwasher. "I'm not sure what it is, but I intend to find out."

* * *

You staying away isn't what I wanted. What did that mean? Cedrick wondered while he laid on the couch in the family room, gazing at the spot where his mom and Mitch had their not so private conversation. *I've been miserable all these years.* What exactly was Mitch unhappy about? And what did his father have to do with any of it?

Cedrick glanced down at his watch and deeply sighed. It was almost one am, but he couldn't wait any longer. He needed answers.

Grabbing his phone from the coffee table, Cedrick dialed Victoria's number.

"Hey, Vicki. I know it's late, but——"

"It's alright. I'm up packing. Is everything okay?"

"Yeah—— no—— not really."

"What is it?" she asked with concern. "I know it's been years since you've confided in me, but I'm still here when you need me, and it looks like this is one of those times."

Still the same Vicki.

After a brief silence, Cedrick said, "There's a lot of things about me that you aren't aware of, Vicki. Certain things have happened and—— please don't take this the wrong way, I wasn't sure if I could trust you."

"I'm not sure how to feel about that."

"Hear me out for a minute," Cedrick insisted. "You dropped in town out of nowhere, and your father-in-law just happens to be Sierra's boss. Then you show up at my house; got angry after our conversation," he whispered, glancing over his shoulder. "Then kissed me and stormed out. Next thing I know, my wife invited you to dinner. All of that transpired within seven days. What am I supposed to think?"

"Well, damn, Cedrick. When you say it like that; it does sound like a conspiracy." She released a hearty laugh. "But I was equally surprised to run into you at the restaurant. I'd always wondered what happened to you and where you'd been. Then I run into your wife in Edward's office of all places. Sierra's a sweetheart, but she wasn't that day. She murdered me ten times over with an icy glare and sharp tongue."

"That sounds like my baby," Cedrick commented, and the corners of his lips turned upward. "She goes hard for her family."

"She's protective of you, and that's good. You need someone like that in your corner."

"Sierra's so good to and for me—— that's why I'm going to tell her about that kiss," he said in a low voice. "I don't want to keep anything from her."

"Don't do that, Cedrick," Victoria implored. "I was emotional and stupid. It never should've happened. Don't cause Sierra any unnecessary pain over a kiss that meant nothing. I'm sorry that I put you in that predicament."

"Babe," Sierra called out from a distance. "When are you coming to bed?"

"Soon, honey. I'll be up in ten," Cedrick responded, shifting to a sitting position.

"I'll let you go. Our flight leaves at six, and I have to finish packing. I'm glad you called though; I've missed talking to you."

"Hold on, Vicki. Don't hang up," Cedrick said hurriedly. "I have something to ask you."

"What's up?"

"Is there anything going on between our parents? I know you saw what I saw. A blind man could see the connection. It definitely appeared to be more than two old friends catching up. Right??"

"I noticed that, too, but I don't know about them ever having a relationship. My dad's quite fond of your mother. I didn't realize how much she meant to him until we started talking about old times and his eyes lit up every time he mentioned her name. It's possible he's sweet on her. Why are you asking?"

"I overheard them talking, and it struck me as strange. I didn't know they were attracted to each other."

"Dad was excited to come to Chicago with me, but he didn't know your mom would be here. He was ecstatic to see you," Victoria said in a cheerful tone. "As am I. I've missed our friendship."

"Same here," he admitted. "I'm glad we've had the chance to reconnect."

Cedrick wanted to express how sorry he was for leaving like that, but that would mean he'd have to explain *why* they'd gone. He refused to bring Victoria into that madness, especially now that he knew in his gut that she didn't know what happened.

"You never told me why you moved?"

"It's complicated," he replied while rubbing his hand over his goatee. "Can we rebuild our friendship starting from where we are today, and leave the past in the past? Is that possible?"

Cedrick could hear her breathing on the other end of the phone. He prayed Victoria would be able to do what he asked because he would very much like to renew their friendship.

"I can do that, even though you're holding out on me. I'm sure you'll tell me one day, but I don't ever want to lose touch again so from this day forward, we're cool."

"Thanks for understanding," Cedrick said with a smile. "Have a safe flight. Let me get off this phone before Sierra calls me again. Bye, Vicki."

Cedrick disconnected the call and headed toward the bedroom. He felt confident that things between him and Victoria were on the upswing, but he still needed answers. So, he had no other choice than to confront his mom.

Chapter 12

"Okay mom, it's been two days now, and I've been waiting for an explanation, but you've been tight-lipped," Cedrick said, walking along Priscilla's side as she rode in a motorized scooter. They were in a department store inside River Oaks Mall, Christmas shopping for Sierra and the girls, taking advantage of the post-Thanksgiving sales. "So, it's time you told me what's going on?"

Instantly, Priscilla looked uncomfortable, stopping the scooter and shifting in the seat. "I don't know what you mean, son."

"I don't think that's true, mom. I need to know. Did you and Mitch have an affair?"

Priscilla's eyes widened. "How dare you ask me that? What kind of woman do you think I am?" She glanced around the department store. "And we're out in public. What if someone heard you?"

"Mom——"

"And if I did, it would be none of your business," she said, her tone sharp and indignant. "I'm a grown woman. I don't need to keep you in the loop on everything I do."

"I'm sorry," Cedrick apologized. "I just… I can't get the image out of my head."

"What image?" she asked, zooming the scooter out of the store toward a sitting area along the Santa Claus workshop display.

"When I told Carrington that my dad died," he whispered, scanning the area. "Victoria was genuinely shocked, but Mitch—— he appeared." Cedrick rubbed his goatee. "I don't know what he seemed, but it wasn't the response I expected."

Priscilla gazed at several kids playing in the distance. She kept silent.

Cedrick let out an exasperated sigh. "Mom. What aren't you telling me?"

"It's nothing you need to worry about, okay," Priscilla reassured, getting to her feet. "I promise you, as much of a jerk as your father was, I did not cheat on him, with Mitch or anyone else."

Cedrick nodded but refrained from commenting that she hadn't exactly answered the question.

* * *

Later that evening, Cedrick received a phone call from Victoria. His eyes lit up when her name flashed across the screen, the same way they did when she knocked on the door when they were kids to see if Cedrick could come out to play. He didn't realize until now, how much he missed his best friend and was grateful for the reconnection.

"Hey, Vicki."

She sobbed into the phone. "My father died this morning."

Cedrick sunk into the bedroom recliner. "What? No," he replied in anguish. "Vicki, I'm so sorry."

"And I can't reach Lennox," she wailed into the phone. "I'm all alone. I don't know what to do."

"Breathe, Vicki," Cedrick said in a soothing tone. "I'm here. You're not alone."

Several awkward moments passed as Victoria cried into the phone. Cedrick listened in companionable silence, intent to remain on the call for as long as she needed him. Many times, Victoria was his place of refuge and comfort. This was the least he could do to repay her kindness and support.

Finally, she composed herself. She cleared her throat a few times before trying to speak. Her voice was little above a deep croak. "This was so sudden. I just spoke to him last night. We had such a great time with your family for Thanksgiving, and he was looking forward to visiting again at Christmas. Please let your mom know." She sniffled. "I'll be in touch with the arrangements. I hope you're all able to come."

Cedrick covered the receiver, closing his eyes. He wanted to be there for Victoria, but he did not want to set foot in Reno.

"Of course, I want to be there for you, Vicki. Honestly, it depends on what's happening with The Smokehouse. Get me the arrangements as soon as possible."

"Okay. Bye, Cedrick."

He heard the disappointment in her voice at his lack of commitment. He felt horrible. What kind of friend was he, putting his needs before hers? Cedrick knew that no matter what, Victoria would stand by him if the truth were discovered, but the old neighborhood was a different story. People talk, and they had long memories at the most inopportune times. He couldn't put his family at risk.

Cedrick was in the middle of dialing his mother on the phone when Sierra entered the bedroom with a massive bowl of popcorn and two sweet teas.

"I get to pick the movie tonight," she insisted, placing the bottles on the nightstand, gazing at her husband. She immediately frowned. "What's wrong?"

"Mitch died."

"Noooo. He was just here a few days ago." Sierra placed the bowl on the bed and walked over and sat in his lap. "Are you okay?"

"I'm numb. I was talking about Mitch earlier with mom. She'd been mad at me for asking inappropriate questions about the two of them—— now this."

"Does Priscilla know?"

"I was in the middle of calling her," Cedrick said, lifting the phone receiver again.

"I'll give you some privacy." She stuck her hand in the popcorn bowl and popped several kernels into her mouth. "I'll go call and check on Victoria. If you need me, I'll be downstairs."

"Thanks, sweetheart."

Taking a deep breath, Cedrick called his mother. Regardless of what Priscilla said, it was evident that she cared for Mitch in more than a neighborly way.

"Hey, mom."

There was a long pause, and then Priscilla said, "Cedrick, why do you sound like that?"

"Sorry about earlier," he said, massaging his temple and trying to buy some time before dropping the bad news.

"It's forgotten as long as you don't bring it up again," she remarked. "Now, quit beating around the bush and tell me what's happened."

"Mom … Mitch passed away, today."

"Dear God," Priscilla moaned, "We talked last night. He laughed and joked as if he didn't have a care in the world. I can't believe he's gone."

Cedrick listened to his mother struggling for composure. His heart ached for her.

"How's Victoria?" she finally replied. "Is she okay?"

"No. She's barely managing. It's so sudden. For everyone, but especially Vicki," Cedrick said, running a hand across his jaw. "I feel bad that she's dealing with this alone. With his hectic schedule, Lennox is rarely at home. Let's hope he can free up his time to help his wife deal with this sudden loss."

"When's the funeral?"

"I don't know. Vicki said she'd let me know as soon as everything's set."

"Good. You can take a couple of days off, and we'll fly over. Victoria's husband's a pilot. I'm sure we can get some tickets at a discount. Especially since there's a death in the family. Granted, we're not exactly family, but—"

Cedrick took a deep breath and plunged into the deep end. "I'm not going."

"What? You can't be serious," Priscilla questioned. "You have to go. Victoria needs all the support she can get right now. And you're her best friend, remember? Why wouldn't you be there for her?"

"I'm not comfortable being there with all the folks from the neighborhood," Cedrick expressed in a shaky voice. "And Mitch's a cop. The entire police force is going to be there. Too many eyes—— I can't risk it, mom. Something could go wrong."

"How many times do I have to tell you, Cedrick." Priscilla sighed, clearly exasperated. "You don't have anything to worry about. You're safe. We're safe."

Cedrick shook his head as if she could see him. "I wish you wouldn't be so cavalier about your safety, but if you insist on going, I'll take you to the airport and set up your hotel and rental car while you're there."

"You aren't going to evade your responsibility to Mitch, or Victoria. That's not the kind of son I raised. They were there for you. Particularly Mitch. More than you'll ever know. Especially toward the end."

"What does that even mean? Mom, I know there are things you aren't telling me. You can deny it all you want, but you're keeping secrets from me," Cedrick countered. "I can feel it. And I'm not getting off this phone until you come clean."

Cedrick could hear his mother's uneven breathing over the phone line. It was the last thing he heard before the line disconnected.

Chapter 13

"Will you stop looking over your shoulder? You're starting to make me paranoid," Sierra whispered.

Cedrick stopped and tried to relax the tense look on his face. "Thanks for coming with me," he said to Sierra, while speed walking through Reno-Tahoe International Airport.

"I've always wanted to visit Nevada," Sierra commented, trying her best to keep up with the rapid pace Cedrick had set.

When they finally arrived at baggage claim, she sat down and tried to catch her breath while they waited for their luggage to arrive. "Granted, I'd always thought it would be Las Vegas we'd visit, but I guess Reno will have to do."

"We could always drive down. We're only six and a half to seven hours away."

"I'm going to hold you to that," Sierra shot back as Cedrick plucked their suitcases from the revolving belt.

Cedrick missed the funeral. He wanted to be there, but he couldn't bring himself to do that; too many old faces would have too many questions that he wasn't prepared to answer. He was grateful that he was able to spend some quality time with Mitch before he died.

The following week after the funeral, Victoria insisted that Cedrick come to Reno for the reading of her father's will. That didn't make any sense to him whatsoever, but he had agreed. He'd let Victoria down once; he wasn't going to do it again.

"I can see the wheels turning," Sierra commented, walking alongside Cedrick to the rental car facility. "What's on your mind?"

He glanced down at his wife. She was stylish in a white puffer coat with matching fur earmuffs. Sierra was all set to wear a tank top, jean shorts, and sandals, until Cedrick informed her that it was just as cold in Reno as it was in Chicago, maybe a tad bit colder during December.

"A lot. Right now, I'm trying to figure out why Mitch would leave me anything?"

"I don't know, but we'll find out soon enough," Sierra remarked.

Cedrick halted, gently pulling Sierra to the side, allowing the people behind them to pass. "What if it's a set-up?" he asked, searching her eyes for answers. "It's like I'm being sucked into a vortex. I *had* to come here. Vicki couldn't, should I say *wouldn't* give me any information over the phone." He stroked his beard. "She *insisted* as if I didn't have a choice."

"Baby, it's too late to second guess this," Sierra said, laying her hand on his chest. "We're already here, besides we're going to Mitch's house. It's only going to be us, Lennox, the attorney, and anyone else that Mitch had named in his will. It's not like the whole town's going to be there like at the funeral."

"I don't know," Cedrick expressed in a whisper. "Too much is at stake."

"Mitch was good to you, right?"

"Always," Cedrick replied. "He was more of a father to me than my dad ever was. You saw for yourself how warm and caring Mitch was. He'd been that way my whole life."

"Then there's a strong possibility that he did leave something for you," Sierra prodded, sliding her hand in his, tugging him forward. "But even if he didn't, Victoria needs her best friend close by, someone, who *really* knew her dad. And besides, your mother keeps saying that you don't have anything to worry about." She squeezed Cedrick's hand. "Maybe it's time you believed her. She came to the funeral and made it back home unscathed."

"I can't believe you're okay with this," he said, shaking his head at his amazing wife.

"Don't fool yourself. I had reservations, but once we discussed everything and after Thanksgiving, I'm cool. I know Victoria's not a threat to our family."

An hour later, they arrived at Victoria's childhood home, parking directly in front of Cedrick's house of horrors next door. He glared out the window; his jaw tightened just taking in his old home. He closed his eyes and tried to control his runaway heartbeat.

"Babe, are you okay?"

Opening his eyes, Cedrick glared upon the time capsule. The same gravel and reddish mulch adorned the front yard. The white aluminum screen door with the mesh torn in the bottom corner had rusted by the handle, and the crescent moon and star wind chime that hung over the side-drive garage door, dangled by a thread.

"There's still no love here," Cedrick mumbled, putting on his hat and getting out of the car. "It looks exactly the same."

"Nothing in there can hurt you anymore," Sierra reminded him, clasping the handles of her purse.

"I know," he replied, scanning the area. "Still, I never thought I'd have to see this house again."

An orange convertible BMW Roadster pulled into Victoria's driveway. A man exited the vehicle with a spiked crew-cut fade, wearing khaki cargo pants and a puffer vest over a black sweater, carrying two bags of ice.

"Lennox," Sierra called out.

"Hi, Sierra," he responded, walking toward them. "I haven't seen you since we interned for my father the summer before I got married."

"This is my husband, Cedrick."

The men exchanged handshakes.

"Sorry I couldn't make it for Thanksgiving. The friendly skies aren't so friendly to the people who work for them," Lennox snickered. "It's nice to put a face with the name finally. I've been hearing about you and Tori's middle school adventures for years."

"I bet," Cedrick replied, glancing at Sierra who stood off to the side with a somber look on her face.

"Let's go inside; it's cold out here." Lennox stepped aside, allowing them to walk the pathway to the front door. "It's open."

Cedrick squeezed Sierra's shoulders from behind. He leaned over and asked, "You good?"

She nodded, walking into the front room.

Flowers, cards, and photo albums were stacked on the floor and coffee table. The casket flag lay, folded atop the fireplace mantle with various awards.

Everything Mitch Weiss represented—— Security. Warmth. Love. Laughter was in that room. That familiarity enveloped Cedrick. He hated himself for not attending Mitch's funeral.

"In the kitchen," a voice yelled from the rear of the house.

Cedrick grabbed one of the bags of ice from Lennox as they made their way into the moderately sized kitchen.

"Heyyyy," Victoria greeted with a smile, hugging Cedrick and then Sierra. "I'm glad you both made it." She walked over to the table and removed several boxes from the chairs. "Please excuse the mess, so much has been going on over the past couple of weeks. Housework is the last thing on my mind," Victoria admitted handing a couple of boxes to Lennox. "Make yourself comfortable."

"The updated kitchen is nice," Cedrick commented, admiring the stainless-steel appliances and granite countertops.

"Thank you," Victoria replied, adding ice to the crystal beverage dispenser. "It only took a leaky ceiling and mold for daddy to get it done. I'd been asking him to modernize it for years."

"It's beautiful," Sierra chimed in, placing her purse on the back of the chair.

Lennox returned, and everyone moved into the adjoining enclosed heated deck and enjoyed fresh squeezed lemonade, fruit, and party sandwiches. Victoria and Cedrick reminisced about the good ole' days of playing the dozens, secret crushes that weren't so secret, and old acquaintances from middle school.

The proximity of being next door to his childhood home escaped Cedrick as he relished the connection with his best friend, wife, and her husband. He wished that they could have lived near each other in their adult life. He envisioned double dates, days at the gym hooping, or shooting pool at the local tavern, and going on a couple's retreat and other joint vacations. It pained him how things had turned out, how fate was sealed for him based on the heat of one moment in time.

An hour later, Lennox excused himself. He and a few pilot friends were spending the weekend in Las Vegas for their annual boy's trip. Victoria walked him out and returned with a previously sealed envelope with Uwezo Omari written across the front.

"I have a confession to make," Victoria said, curling her legs to the side as she sat on the loveseat across from Cedrick and Sierra. "There's no reading of the will."

Cedrick leaned forward. A myriad of emotions crossing his face before he said, "Vicki, what's this about?"

"I do have something for you, but—— I thought it was best to wait until Lennox was gone," Victoria said, handing an envelope to Cedrick. "As much as I hate keeping secrets from my husband, this wasn't my secret to tell and—— I'm sure you didn't want anyone to know this."

"You read it?" Sierra gasped, examining the torn seal.

"I found this in daddy's file while searching for his life insurance papers," Victoria admitted, shifting in the seat. "I didn't know what it was. Curiosity got the better of me." Victoria covered her mouth. For a moment, she was overcome with sadness. Eventually, she said,

"I'm sorry … about everything."

Cedrick glanced at Sierra, and she looped her arm in his, laying her head on his bicep. He gazed at Victoria, the sorrow in her eyes mirrored his in an unspoken language of their own.

What's in this letter?

Several minutes passed. Cedrick read the letter three times before he'd allow himself to believe the words printed on the paper. His eyes welled with tears, his heart burned with rage, and his brain overloaded with confusion.

"My father's alive."

Chapter 14

"How's this possible?" Cedrick blurted, blinking away the moisture pooling in his eyes. "He couldn't have survived …"

Sierra took the letter from his twitching fingers and read it. Glancing at Victoria, she asked, "When did you find out about this?"

"A couple of weeks ago while going through my father's things. I didn't know any of this." She sipped her lemonade nervously. "… it explains your disappearance."

He took the letter from Sierra and reread it, flashing back to that horrid afternoon.

* * *

Cedrick raided the refrigerator after school, hoping there was some leftover spaghetti. Much to his liking, there was. He slurped the noodles and checked his MySpace account while listening to music through oversized headphones that tuned out the rest of the world.

Priscilla nudged him, whizzing by with her hijab in hand. "You could've got the door. I'm expecting a package."

"Ma." Cedrick removed the headphones, after devouring another forkful of spaghetti. "I got it."

"I'm here now," she yelled, huffing.

Cedrick put the headphones back on and cranked up the volume.

One minute later, his father stormed pass with the Quran tucked under his arm, heading toward the front room. Cedrick didn't think anything of the swift movement. He was just happy that the object of his dad's annoyance wasn't him. It wasn't until the Lil Wayne track switched, causing a three-second gap of silence between songs that Cedrick heard his mother's curdling screams.

Cedrick snatched the headphones off and grabbed the closest weapon. Sprinting to the front room, he froze at the sight of his father stomping his mother in the face as he accused her of disrespecting him. Many times, Cedrick had been beaten by that madman, but he'd never laid a hand on his mother. Never.

"Get off her," Cedrick shrieked with tears flowing down his cheeks, clutching the fork in his fist.

"Oh, so this gets a rise out of you," Haashim growled. "It's your fault that she went to the door without her hijab in the first place," he spat. "Too busy listening to that hippity-hoppity music."

Cedrick's chest heaved in short spurts. If he didn't know any better, he'd swear he was having an asthma attack. He wasn't asthmatic.

"You should be studying this," Hasshim shouted, pointing to the Quran. "Instead of——" Hasshim's face contorted into a form Cedrick hadn't seen before, then he kicked Priscilla in the stomach, then reared back to drive his fist into her face, but he caught a fork to the neck instead.

For years, his dad had been itching for a response from Cedrick; a wail, a cry; anything that showed Hasshim's dominance over his son. Well, he got a response. Not the one he'd been seeking, but the one he deserved.

* * *

Cedrick shuttered out of the dreadful memory. Bolting off the couch, he announced, "I have to call my mom." He dug the car keys out of his pocket and took determined strides out of the room.

"Where are you going?" Sierra questioned, scurrying behind him with Victoria on her heels.

"I can't be here," Cedrick shouted with aggression.

"Baby," Sierra said softly, trying to grab his hand, but Cedrick pulled away. "Where are you going?" she repeated. "I'm worried about you."

"I just need some air," he replied, opening the door.

"Cedrick——" Sierra pleaded, "Please be careful."

"Let him go," Victoria said, clasping Sierra's upper arms. "He'll be alright. He needs a minute to digest this."

* * *

The noise in Cedrick's mind kept up enough raucous of its own, so he drove in silence, forty-five minutes out of Reno on the open road along the Burner Byway, making his first stop at Pyramid Lake.

Crisp air swirled around Cedrick's face and filled his lungs as he breathed in the tranquility. The panoramic view of snow-covered pyramids appeared as if they floated over the blue glacier water, unbothered. This was where he needed to be to face his new reality—— a place where peace outweighed the chaos of life.

The devil was alive, and he couldn't help but think his father had survived for no other reason than to spite him. Cedrick understood why Mitch went to such lengths—— protecting him the way a real father should, making sure Cedrick couldn't be labeled as a murderer, making sure he didn't have a felony hanging over his head for the rest of his life, giving him a chance at normalcy, and never having the opportunity to seek closure from the man who helped create him. If only he'd told him.

Mitch knew the whole time that Cedrick was being abused. Cedrick wasn't sure how to feel about that shocking piece of information, even though Mitch explained why. Priscilla begged Mitch not to arrest his dad. How could he know and not do anything to stop it, regardless of her request? Deep down he knew Mitch did what he felt was right, and Cedrick appreciated Mitch looking out for him the best way he knew how, but his mother knew all along that his father was alive. Why on earth didn't she tell him?

Walking along the iced-over shoreline, Cedrick dialed his mother.

"Hey, son," Priscilla answered in a cheerful tone. "How's——"

"My dad's alive." Cedrick paused, pulling the skullcap over his ears. "And you didn't tell me."

The silence on the other end of the phone was the loudest confirmation.

"Mom."

"Yes," she said in a raspy tone, clearing her throat.

"Why would you keep that from me?" Cedrick asked, rocking back and forth.

"How'd you find out?"

"Really? That's the best you can do by way of confirmation?" Cedrick snapped.

He blew out a harsh breath, watching it dance in the frigid air.

"Cedrick, please tell me," his mother implored.

"Mitch left a note, detailing how he helped *you* cover-up what actually happened to dad and my involvement." He hesitated, dragging his boots along the crunchy ice. "Mitch said he patched dad up, then dropped him off across state lines in Sierra County, California at the hospital as a John Doe."

"I *wanted* you to have a clean start," Priscilla admitted. "With Haashim around, you never would've blossomed into the man you are today. I went to Mitch for help after I dropped you off at Aunt

Makayla's house. I didn't know what to do—— I couldn't physically move him," she cried. "Mitch insisted on getting him medical attention. He promised that we would be safe. I couldn't chance the truth coming out, so I packed you up, and we left. Simple as that."

That was a finality phrase that Priscilla used when she was done with a conversation. Cedrick typically respected it, but there were too many unanswered questions that only his mother could answer.

"Only that wasn't the end of the story, was it, mom? Why didn't you tell me as you promised in the letter when I turned twenty-one? Is this what you and Mitch were whispering about on Thanksgiving?"

"Yes," Priscilla confessed. "He was shocked that you didn't know. I didn't want him to say anything because I knew Victoria didn't know anything about it and it would've confused Carrington who'd always thought her other grandfather was dead."

"So, did her father," he shot back. "But that doesn't explain why you didn't tell me the truth."

"There wasn't a need at first," Priscilla explained. "Your father wasn't doing well, and I thought he might succumb to his injuries."

"Wait," Cedrick said, standing as still as the rock formations. "You were checking in on him?"

"No, Mitch was," Priscilla explained. "He kept me abreast of everything."

"Oh, this keeps getting better and better," he said dryly.

"Now, let me finish," she said, annoyance clear in her tone. "As Hasshim improved, Mitch made living arrangements for him in Sierra County, paying his rent for one year. He made him promise never to contact us again, return to Nevada, or speak of what happened that afternoon. If he did, Mitch would have him arrested for domestic assault and battery. He'd lose his freedom and be shunned in the Muslim community forever."

Silence hung in the air.

In a softer voice, Priscilla further explained, "You had just completed culinary school and met Sierra. Son, you were so happy—— I couldn't drag a never-ending rain cloud over your sunshine."

"But that's just what I had," he said hotly. "All these years, you let me believe I killed him. We ..." Cedrick mumbled, digging his shoes in the snow. "I've been living in fear my entire life since that incident, and you had the power to make it stop, yet you didn't."

"I told you there wasn't anything to worry about."

"That's your excuse for the nightmare I've been living? That doesn't begin to explain everything. You telling me not to worry about it were just hollow words without the facts to back them up," Cedrick shot back, louder than he would normally address his mother. He felt bad, but his anger had been let out of its cage now, and it was hard getting it back under control. "Can't you see this nightmare I've been living in has redirected my whole life?"

"And look who you've become," she bragged in a matter-of-fact tone. "A well-known chef who owns your restaurant, a homeowner of prime real estate in Lincoln Park before the age of thirty, with a beautiful wife who adores you, and two loving daughters. I will *not* apologize for the decisions I've made for our family."

"At what cost?" He railed aloud. "My sanity? Was it worth it, mom? Were the secrets you kept from me really worth my peace of mind?"

Chapter 15

Cedrick ended the call with Priscilla. He screamed to the top of his lungs and listened to his voice echo off the lake and the pyramids. Cedrick walked the open land until his fingers were numb and couldn't feel his face.

Shoving gloved hands in his pockets, he jogged back to the car, still shocked at what he learned. Now, what was he supposed to do? Sierra County, California was a little over an hour away. Cedrick knew this because Mitch took Cedrick skiing there with his family once over winter break. He had the best time, in part because he got a reprieve from dealing with his father.

Cedrick started the engine and cranked the heat to the highest setting, cupping his hands together and blowing warm breath on them. As the red hue returned to his flesh, Cedrick lifted his phone. He had several missed calls from Sierra and Victoria.

He called his wife.

"Oh my gosh, Cedrick. Where are you? Are you okay?"

"Slow down, baby. I'm fine," he assured, rubbing his hands

together. "At least physically, anyway."

"Please come back to the house," Sierra pleaded. "I need to put my eyes on you."

"Not yet, but soon." He splayed his fingers in front of the vents. "Could you get that letter?"

"Sure."

Cedrick listened as papers ruffled in the background. Those few seconds gave him clarity. He had to follow through, or he'd live with regret for the rest of his life. The *what if's* would continue to haunt him.

"I got it," Sierra said, coming back to the phone.

"What's Haashim's address and phone number?"

"Wait. Cedrick, what are you about to do?" Sierra inquired, waiting for her husband's response.

"I have to see him for myself, Sierra. I have to put this all to rest."

"Come get me. I'll go with you," Sierra implored. "You don't have to do this alone."

"I know I don't, but I feel I have to," he replied. "I'll be fine, sweetheart. I'll call you when I make it there. I love you."

* * *

There's no going back now. Cedrick mused as he pulled up to a structure that resembled a country club but was actually an assisted living facility for seniors. The landscaping was immaculate; the oversized green awning had gold monogrammed letters that beamed like Batman's signal in the sky; the place screamed money.

Cedrick whistled aloud. It would seem his father had landed on his feet. "Not too shabby," Cedrick said as he walked inside and approached the front desk. "Hello, I'm here to visit Brian Dalton."

"Who?" the older gentleman asked, glancing up at him from behind his thick frames.

Cedrick brows knitted. He knew he entered the correct address into the navigation system. "Brian Dalton," he repeated, pulling out his phone to call Sierra for verification.

"I'm sorry, there isn't a Brian Dalton listed in our database. There's another assisted living facility seven miles from here."

"Thank you," Cedrick replied, heading for the exit.

Suddenly, he stopped short. Maybe this was a sign. He texted Sierra to ask for confirmation of the address. She texted the exact address that he'd entered into the navigation app on his phone earlier.

Cedrick sighed. It had been fifteen years. It's possible his father had moved on or died. Either way, the possibility that he wasn't getting any answers today didn't sit well with him.

He sulked, trudging back to his car, not sure why he was sad when The Words of the Adhan pierced the air over a loudspeaker. The Islamic call to prayer had just begun. Cedrick glanced at his watch, his head snapping upward toward the sun, remembering Islamic teaching as if it were yesterday. Nodding, he uttered, "late afternoon prayer." He Googled mosques near me. Two seconds later, a mosque appeared, point seven miles away on the screen. His father was undoubtedly at this facility.

What was he thinking asking for Brian Dalton? His dad wore his given name like a badge of honor, though he'd never been an honorable man.

Cedrick went back inside. "I'm sorry to keep bothering you, sir. I'm here to visit Haashim Muhammad."

"Sign in, please," the man instructed. He handed Cedrick a visitor's pass. "Room 213, but you'll have to wait about fifteen minutes or so, he's in the middle of prayer."

"No problem."

* * *

Cedrick waited in the community room. He welcomed the company of strangers; they kept his mind from wandering. The joy on their faces was evident as they spent time with loved ones and other residents, playing cards, knitting, and working crossword puzzles together.

He never had that kind of interaction with Haashim. His dad wasn't interested in anything outside of Islam. Why was this meeting important? Cedrick didn't know why he was so adamant about finding his dad or what he'd say once they were face to face. The letter wasn't enough. Cedrick needed visual confirmation that the man was alive. He'd figure out the rest as it unfolded.

Pulling out his phone, he dialed Priscilla. "I'm in Sierra County, California. Dad's in an assisted living facility right across the Nevada border."

The line was so quiet that Cedrick thought the call dropped.

"Mom. Are you there?"

"Son." Priscilla sighed. "I'm not sure what you're after—— Absolution? Acceptance? I don't know, but I want you to be prepared if those things don't happen. I need you to be okay—— for yourself and your family. Do you understand what I'm saying?"

"I do."

"You're a good man, in spite of your upbringing and you are a doting father. Don't lose sight of that or who you are, searching for something you may never find."

"I hear you, ma," Cedrick replied, "I know you're trying to protect me now as you did then, but you still should've told me and let me decide for myself."

Priscilla didn't utter a sound.

"I have to go," Cedrick said, noting the shift in the sun. "I love you."

Cedrick took the stairs to the second level to give himself more time to gather his thoughts. Room 213 was directly across from the stairwell. He glanced in each direction down the hall. The place resembled a hotel with a line of doors, industrial carpeting, and crystal light fixtures.

He rapped on the half-open door, before entering. When he stepped in, he saw a man in pale blue scrubs assisting his father off the floor and folded his prayer carpet.

"Haashim, you have a visitor."

The older man turned around slowly with the help of a walker. "Who are you kidding Akbar, no one visits me."

"Hello, dad."

Both men turned toward Cedrick.

"I didn't know you had a son," Akbar said, holding Haashim by the arm until he steadied himself. "Come in, As-salamu alaykum."

"Wa-Alaykum al-salaam," Cedrick returned the greeting of peace unto you, stepping further into the room.

Less than a minute in his presence and Cedrick fell into an old routine by returning the Islamic greeting. He could've just said, hello. He gazed into his father's eyes. They were cold, just the way Cedrick remembered them, but with a hint of sadness.

Akbar helped Haashim ease onto the recliner. "Let me know if you need anything," he said before leaving and pulling up the door.

"I wasn't sure I'd ever see you again," his father admitted, glaring at Cedrick who stood firm, mere inches from the exit.

"Same here."

"I know you didn't come here to stare at me," Hasshim snorted, pressing the buttons on the side of the recliner. "What do you want?"

The feeling of tiny needles pricked every nerve in Cedrick's body. He clenched his teeth so hard they throbbed. His father was the same cantankerous man he'd always been. His body may be broken, but his tongue still cut sharper than a sword.

"Nothing." Cedrick turned to leave. "This was a mistake."

"Boy don't walk away when I'm talking to you," Haashim's voice boomed, paralyzing Cedrick's movement.

Cedrick balled his fist, trying to contain the blazing anger inside of him. "I'm a grown man, and you *will* respect me."

Letting out a throaty chuckle, his father said, "Get on out of here, then." Dismissing Cedrick with the wave of a hand. "You're not worth my time."

Reaching for the TV remote, Haashim turned his attention to the show on the screen.

"What did I ever do for you to treat me this way?" Cedrick asked, crossing his arms. "Why don't you love me?"

Flicking the channels, he ignored Cedrick's question.

Cedrick had enough of his father's theatrics. He charged forward, snatching the remote from his father's hand. Haashim attempted to raise his arm up and away from his son, but gravity yanked his frail frame back down.

"What did I do to deserve a father like you?"

"I took pity on my wife's bastard son," he smirked, staring defiantly at Cedrick. "You weren't mine. You were just a problem I inherited."

"Come again?" Cedrick said as an electric current surged through his body. The shock was keeping him rooted to his spot.

"That's right," Haashim spat, his eyes flashed with anger. "I'm not your biological father."

"You're a liar," Cedrick growled in his father's face. He was so close they could have kissed. "You'd say anything to hurt me."

"Ask your mother."

Cedrick stood to his full height and glowered at the man who raised him. Hasshim was a monster from a special breed. As much as Cedrick wanted to discredit his paternal lineage, he had a feeling it was true. He wouldn't have brought Priscilla into the mix if it wasn't.

"So, why be bothered if I wasn't your child?"

"Because I loved your mother," he replied matter-of-factly, tapping a wrinkled finger on the chair arm. "I tried to love you, but you wouldn't conform. You always had something to say; wouldn't stop asking questions. You needed to learn who was the head of the household."

"And that made it okay for you to beat me?" Cedrick snapped, tossing the remote in Haashim's lap.

"You needed to learn discipline. As your father, my rules weren't to be questioned."

"The only thing I learned from you is how *not* to be. Honestly, I'm relieved I'm not your son; that your DNA isn't flowing through my veins." Cedrick eyed the stranger before him with contempt. "You don't ever have to worry about seeing or hearing from me again. The son you didn't want."

"Close the door on your way out," Haashim countered. He turned his attention back to flicking the channels on the remote.

Cedrick rushed to the exit, then grabbed the doorknob. He took one last glance over his shoulder and narrowed his eyes. "May Allah have mercy on your soul, because I never will."

Chapter 16

Cedrick stumbled out into the parking lot and doubled over, placing his hands on his knees for support. His breathing was choppy. He should've listened to his mother and left things as they were. He gained nothing, but new heartache, going to see his father. *Or who he thought was his father.* His mind corrected. How could one man be so hateful?

"There he is." Cedrick heard a familiar voice say. His head snapped up from between his legs. The rapid movement almost caused a crook in his neck. That's when he spotted Sierra running toward him with Victoria close on her heels.

When she reached his side, Sierra threw her arms around him. "Are you okay," she asked panting, reaching up and cupping his cheeks. "I've been worried sick."

"I'm glad you're here," he said, trying to tamp down the alternating anger, nausea, and shock he felt at Haashim's declaration. "Both of you," he said including Victoria. "Let's go. I need to get as far away from this place as possible," Cedrick remarked, he spared a final look at the building from the corner of his eye.

"Everything's in the car. We can head to the airport now if that's what you want," Sierra suggested. She linked their hands together as they headed for the car.

"Yeah … I'm ready to get out of here."

Cedrick approached Victoria. "Thank you for the enlightenment. I wasn't ready for it, but I needed to know."

Tears drifted down her cheeks. "I'm so sorry, Cedrick. For all of it."

He nodded. "Me, too."

"Are we good?" she asked hesitantly.

Giving his best friend a grateful nod, he moved forward and pulled her into his arms. "Always. I appreciate you looking out for me, as usual."

"We'll head to the airport from here," Sierra said, interrupting their embrace. She placed a hand on Victoria's shoulder. "Thanks for looking out for him."

"No sweat," Victoria replied, hugging Sierra. "Take care— both of you."

* * *

The following day, Cedrick went to visit his mother. He didn't feel comfortable asking the type of questions he needed answers for over the phone. So, without warning, he showed up at Priscilla's house.

"Hey, son," she said with a solemn expression. "I've been expecting you."

Cedrick stared in a daze. How did she know he was coming to visit?

"Don't look so surprised. I knew you'd come." Priscilla stepped aside to let him enter.

Cedrick followed his mother into the living room. He plopped down on the couch, but Priscilla perched on the very edge as if she was prepared to take flight at any moment.

"How'd you know that?"

"When I didn't hear back from you after we last talked, I knew you'd spoken with your father. Haashim being the man he is." She took a deep breath and swallowed. "I knew he wouldn't make things easy or probably gave you half-truths." Priscilla tilted her head to the side. "Am I right?"

"That depends on you," he said, crossing his arms.

Suddenly unable to sit still, Priscilla got up. "I was in the middle of cooking breakfast," she called over her shoulder as she headed for the kitchen. She didn't bother checking to see if Cedrick would follow. "You hungry?"

"Not really," he replied as he rose to his feet and strode behind her. He sat down at the table while she finished preparing her meal.

"Nonsense." Priscilla grabbed two additional eggs from the refrigerator. "You need to eat something." She smiled at him. "Scrambled or sunny-side up?"

"Is Haashim my father?"

A crisp crackling sound permeated the air, accompanied by gooey liquid that oozed from Priscilla's closed fist before dropping to the floor. She opened her hand and shook the broken eggshell pieces into the sink. After washing her hands, she claimed a seat next to Cedrick.

"No, he's not," Priscilla confessed, drying her hands on a towel. "I don't know what Haashim told you, but——"

"That he wasn't my father and if I didn't believe him, then to ask you," Cedrick said with a questioning grimace. "Are you going to deny it? Send me off on another quest for truths you could've told me from the beginning?"

She bristled at his stern tone. "My intentions have always been to protect you." Priscilla reached out to stroke his hand, but he shifted away. She took several deep breaths before continuing. "You were conceived in rape."

The chair legs scraped against the floor as Cedrick bolted out of his chair. Priscilla rose to follow him, but he shook his head in warning.

She lowered herself back to her chair.

"Son—"

"Tell me," he whispered in a harsh tone.

"I was a virgin when I met your father. We were young and in love." A slight smile lifted the corners of her mouth for a hot second before being overshadowed with pain and anguish. "The night before we were supposed to sign the Islamic marriage contract, I went out with friends. They insisted on throwing me a bachelorette party, but I begged them not to. Eventually, they gave up, and we hung out at the park across the street from a disco club. The music was so loud that we had to shout to hear each other talk."

Cedrick listened with an acute ear, wondering how a girl's night out resulted in a sexual assault.

"Drunkards spilled out of the club and into the park." Priscilla closed her eyes, biting her lip. "I recognized one of the men. He was the Qadi."

"The who?"

"The Islamic judge who was supposed to marry us," she said, with a quivering voice.

Cedrick remembered learning about the Qadi during a Quran study session with Haashim.

"The Qadi was beyond tipsy, but sober enough to not recognize me." Priscilla paused. A single tear skirted down her cheek. "The Qadi slurred when he summoned me to go inside the club with him. I didn't want to go, but I felt like I didn't have a choice. Once we got close to the building, he pulled me around the back into a dank alley and said, you caught me," referring to his drinking, Priscilla explained. "Then he yanked me so close that I thought I'd vomit from the reeking smell of alcohol. It was everywhere." She shuddered in recollection. "His mouth, clothes, even his skin. He hissed, *Since you have a one-up on me, I need to have a one-up on you to guarantee your silence,*" Priscilla cried, her knee bouncing uncontrollably under the table. "Then … he raped me."

The finality of her story and the pain in her voice was what wrenched Cedrick from his anger-induced haze. Instantly, he sobered and rushed to her side.

"I'm so sorry I made you recount such a horrible crime."

"No, I had to," she choked out. "It was past time you know everything."

"Don't cry, momma," Cedrick comforted, kneeling in front of Priscilla, massaging her twitching hands and wiping her tear stained face.

After gaining her composure, Priscilla continued, "I pushed back the signing of the Islamic marriage contract for three months, contemplating if I was worthy of Haashim's love ... I was no longer pure, and I couldn't tell him what happened. I didn't think he or anyone else would believe me. Who would? It's the Qadi. Then two weeks later, I missed my period."

Cedrick gazed into Priscilla's yielding eyes, realizing she'd been put in an impossible situation.

"I didn't have a choice but to come clean. Haashim swore I was lying to cover up a premarital tryst. Even if that were the case, why would I blame it on an Islamic judge? I'd never dated anyone before your father, so the likeliness of me being with someone, was next to none," Priscilla explained. "About a week after I told him, we were at the market and ran into the Qadi with his family. My bladder involuntarily released, and I remembered waking up on a gurney. When I think about it, I can still feel the warm urine trickling down my legs before they went numb."

Cedrick dropped his head in Priscilla's lap, trying to hold back the tears that had a mind of their own as they spilled onto her housecoat.

"Don't feel sorry for me," she said in a loving tone, rubbing his back. "You're the reason I draw a breath every day. There isn't a mother's love greater than the love I have for you."

"You're a brave woman," Cedrick acknowledged, feeling Priscilla's profession of love deep in his soul.

"I'm a mother," she replied with the first genuine smile she'd had all morning. "It's my job, and the greatest one I've ever known."

Cedrick stood, grabbed paper towels and dishwashing liquid, and cleaned the mess off the floor. "How did you and Haashim end up married? Especially since he didn't believe you?"

"Once I regained consciousness, he scooped me up off the gurney, refusing medical treatment on my behalf. If the paramedic would've examined me, my pregnancy would've been revealed. From that day forward, he promised to protect my secret, claim you as his son, and marry me before I began to show. We signed the contract, and the Qadi performed the short ceremony as if nothing happened. We didn't consummate the marriage until after you were born."

"That sounds like torture," Cedrick remarked, thinking how strong his mother had to be, being married by her rapist, and pretending like everything was alright when she was broken and carrying his child.

"It was one of the best and worst days of my life," she confessed.

"The man who loved you sounds nothing like the one that raised me."

"He tried to love you as his own ... at least in the beginning. I don't think he ever got over how you were conceived, although he knew I was forced, I'd still been with another man," Priscilla reflected, rubbing her arms as if she was cold. "I'm not making any excuses for him, the Haashim I loved, died years ago, and I'm at peace with that," she said, holding onto the table for support as she stood.

"Why didn't you leave?"

"It wasn't that simple, son. As a young Muslim wife, I didn't have any power. Financially, we were dependent on your father—— Haashim. I wasn't allowed to work outside of the home." She frowned, wringing her hands. "Times were very different than they are now. "I'd saved eleven-hundred dollars from the grocery money that I'd been skimming from over the years," Priscilla admitted. "I'd never stolen anything in my life, but I needed access to money of my own. At the time, I didn't know what for, but I'm thankful it was there when the situation arose."

Cedrick gathered her up in his arms. All the animosity he'd felt against her for hiding the truth was long gone. She was his mother——

his greatest defender and he would be the same for her.

"Thanks for loving me enough to keep me," Cedrick said in a voice laced with affection. He rested his chin on her shoulder. "I owe you my life."

"Nonsense," she protested.

"It's true. If not for your courage and love, I wouldn't be here. I'm proud to call you mom and blessed to be your son." Cedrick smiled. "Now, go on and relax. I'll whip up a breakfast fit for a queen."

Epilogue

"I feel free for the first time in my life," Cedrick admitted to Sierra as they peeled from underneath the girls who had fallen asleep on them while watching Princess and the Frog in the family room.

"Where did that come from?"

"I was thinking about everything that has happened these past few months," he replied, looking down at the girls, then back to Sierra. "And now, I can breathe without always looking over my shoulder or over analyzing hang-up calls or wondering if people's intentions are genuine. I can have peace of mind knowing that I owe nothing to the monster that raised me. I can relax and truly be free in my spirit to love you, and the girls and give you the best life possible with a healthy heart and mind," he said, lifting Lena into his arms and stroking her hair. "I'm sorry for the nightmare I put you through."

"No apologies needed. I'm grateful that through all of it, we've grown closer as a couple and our level of understanding has deepened. I'm happy that you know the whole story about your past and finally have closure regarding Haashim. And you've reconnected with

Victoria," Sierra countered, grabbing Carrington by the hand and assisting her to her feet. "I have no regrets. If we had to go through the storm to get to where we are now, it was all worth it."

After tucking the girl's in their beds, Cedrick and Sierra returned to the family room. She picked up the empty popcorn bowls and crumpled napkins, then turned toward the kitchen.

"Leave it," Cedrick said, removing the items from her hands and placing them on the end table. "I'll take care of this mess in the morning. Right now, I need all of your attention," he said, scooping Sierra into his arms as if he were going to carry her over the threshold.

Giggling, Sierra wrapped her arms around his neck. "What're you doing?"

"I love you, Mrs. Dalton," Cedrick whispered, planting a soft kiss on Sierra's lips. "I vow from this day forward to make sure you always feel loved, cherished, and protected. I promised all of these things when we got married, but I need to rededicate my life to you, by being the best me I can be, and the first step is therapy."

"There's nothing sexier than a man who can admit his faults and is willing to do something about them," she said, laying her head on his shoulder. "You have my support."

Lightly shrugging to get her attention, Sierra lifted her head. "I want to make sure you know that I'll never check out on you. To make sure you know, that *I know,* it isn't an option. I will be here, talking your cars off and doing all the things that work your last nerves for the rest of our natural lives."

Sierra slowly ran a finger along the side of his face, tracing his jawbone. "I wouldn't have it any other way."

Their lips met each other's in an intense kiss. When they came up for air, tears had flooded both of their eyes and spilled onto their faces. Cedrick brushed his lips over the salty liquid running down Sierra's cheek while she wiped his away with her thumb.

"I've never felt more connected to you than I do in this moment," Cedrick whispered, gazing into her eyes.

"Same here," she responded, pressing her hand against his heart.

Cedrick pulled her more into him, carrying Sierra into their bedroom. He laid her down on the bed and climbed on top of her.

"What are you doing?" she asked in a flirty tone.

"Do you really have to ask?"

They hadn't been intimate since the suicide attempt. Cedrick didn't want to come to Sierra until he was the best version of himself. He was on his way to becoming that person.

"No—— but." She squirmed in response to the soft nibbles on her neck. "Oh, how I've missed this anddddd as much as I'm enjoying it—— um—— don't start something you can't finish."

Cedrick pushed up on his arms, glancing down at her. "Besides Lena *maybe* waking up for a bottle, what other reason could there be?"

"The grand opening of Le Dalton Brasseur Bistro in less than ten hours."

Cedrick was thrilled that Chef Brasseur accepted his offer to join his staff at The Smokehouse. But after observing Juan in action during his hiatus, Cedrick promoted him to head chef and opened another restaurant. He and Chef Brasseur were now business partners.

"I didn't forget about that."

"I think it's cool what you did for him."

"It was a win for both of us, but I don't want to talk about that right now," Cedrick said under hooded eyes. "I want to make love to my wife."

Sierra's eyelashes fluttered, and a smile spread across her face. "Well, don't let me stop you."

About the Author

National bestselling author, London St. Charles, has always had a passion for the pen, paper, and books. She is a Chicago native who uses the Windy City as a backdrop to the romance, suspense, and contemporary fiction stories she writes. London published her debut novel, *The Husband We Share* in 2017 and is one of nine authors in the anthology, *Sugar*. She's currently working on several bodies of work scheduled to release throughout 2019. In addition, she composes an online newsletter, *London Writes*, that keeps readers abreast of what's going on in her world.

FOLLOW LONDON ON SOCIAL MEDIA
Amazon Author Page: https://www.amazon.com/-/e/B0778SX2RV
Facebook Author Page: https://www.facebook.com/
AuthorLondonStCharles/
Goodreads: https://www.goodreads.com/auth.../.../17310964.London_
St_Charles
BookBub: https://www.bookbub.com/profile/london-st-charles
Instagram: https://www.instagram.com/london_writes/
Twitter: https://twitter.com/LSCharles2017

FIND LONDON ON THE WEB AND SIGN UP FOR LONDON'S
NEWSLETTER
www.londonstcharles.com

Excerpt of
Sugarcoated Deception by London St. Charles

Four words would put an end to Cadence Goldsmith's perfect life.

"That's Mr. Goldsmith, Mommy."

She searched out the source of that small childlike screech, an unnatural occurrence in the Adali Global Reveal. The event was an exclusive affair for people who worked in the European auto market.

Cadence peered around the velvet curtain from her spot backstage of the McCormick Place Convention Center, surprised to find that her husband, Jackson, and mother, Phylicia were sitting in the front row next to a scowling Steven Bekker, her work nemesis.

"Hiiiiiii, Mr. Goldsmith," a little girl with light-brown skin, blue-eyes and puffy blonde twists crooned, as she rushed to stand near her husband. "You work at my school."

Cadence grimaced. Why was a child there and why was she so interested in Jackson? Wait, was that an image of her husband on that child's shirt? She almost couldn't make it out because the girl's fist twisted the material.

"I present to you, CDO, Cadence Goldsmith."

Applause rang out as she strutted center stage with her attention on the bleached-blonde woman wearing a navy dress, who grinned and winked at her before taking an empty seat next to Jackson and pulling the little girl onto her lap. Jackson glanced at Cadence, then frowned as he put his focus back on the woman. She didn't miss the panic that took over his features for a split second.

Cadence's heart surged with a bit of panic of her own. She prayed that her confidence would still show through, even though relishing the acknowledgement of being the designer of the first self-driving automobile was taking a back seat to Jackson and the unknown guests.

Jackson, who seemed occupied with the distraction that little girl had become, hadn't acknowledged Cadence at all. He and the woman were having a heated, but whispered conversation. Jackson's body language—tense and angry—screamed discomfort.

"May I have everyone's attention please," Cadence said walking to the edge of the stage, standing in front of her husband.

Jackson's brown eyes gazed into hers, but the comfort and security she usually felt was missing.

"Mommy, now," the little girl asked.

"Shhhh." The woman placed an index finger to her thin pink lips. "Not yet."

Cadence raised an eyebrow, then glanced at her husband.

The lights dimmed, and Cadence began the PowerPoint presentation of the newest addition to the Adali luxury car fleet.

Ten minutes later, every person, except for Steven and the mystery woman, were on their feet clapping.

Mike lifted a hand to settle the crowd. "Cadence Goldsmith has a bright future with Adali, and we, along with the two most important people in her life, would like to present her with the Outstanding Innovative Design Award."

"Yay, Mr. Goldsmith," the little girl squealed, slapping her hands together. Cadence's attention was drawn to the child whose eyes matched the woman she assumed to be her mother. High heels clicking across the stage accompanied by Jackson's signature fragrance snapped Cadence from the trance.

Mike handed a plaque with the Adali emblem engraved on it to Cadence.

"Thank you." She shook his hand trying to play it cool even though she wanted to shatter the surrounding windows with a high-pitched scream.

"Congratulations." Jackson beamed with cautionary excitement written all over his face as he embraced his wife.

"Who the hell is that woman," she whispered through a clenched-teeth grin as her lips brushed the side of his ear.

Jackson's dark-skin ashen. "Her name's Braelyn," he replied, planting a timid kiss on her cheek. "We'll talk later."

Her mother stepped forward. "Your father would be so proud of you."

Small feet galloping up the stairs onto the stage made everyone in the audience gasp. Cadence peered over Phylicia's shoulder at the lively little girl sprinting forward, spotting a picture of Jackson splayed on the front of her shirt.

Executive's plucked phones from their purses and suit jacket pockets.

Security rushed in. "We're going to have to ask you to get your child and leave, ma'am."

"I have a right to be here," Braelyn exclaimed, throwing a glance at Steven as she flashed the VIP badge.

After a thorough inspection, the guard said with a remorseful tone, "My apologies, Ms. Nevels." He glanced at Mike. "She has clearance."

"Nevels," Cadence whispered, wondering why that name sounded so familiar.

"Show everyone your cute shirt, Jackie," Braelyn instructed, smiling at the pretty girl, before planting a menacing glare at Cadence and Jackson.

Jackie spread her arms wide, facing the audience. "Look, Mommy." She pointed jumping in place. Everybody's taking my picture." She put her hands on her hips and said, "Cheeeeese."

The lump in Cadence's throat grew larger with every word she read on the back of Jackie's shirt.

Jackson Goldsmith Is My Daddy.

Available on Amazon/Kindle Unlimited

Excerpt of
The Husband We Share by London St. Charles

Chapter One

Lauren Carter screamed and bolted upright in her bed, snatched from the reoccurring nightmare that had plagued her for years. She touched a finger to her right ear, expecting to feel a drop of blood, but found none. Damp tendrils of hair clung to her flushed face as she swiped a hand to move them to clear her vision.

"Help me please!"

That voice then, and now, still echoed in Lauren's mind along with the consequences of Lauren's mistake. Hours went by as Lauren was forced to listen to Shawn's shrieks of pain. Trapped on the other side of the door, Lauren was powerless to save the little girl who had come to depend on her for so much.

"You'd better stop screaming, or I'll kill you," a raspy voice had barked. A voice belonging to a complete stranger; a man who'd managed to sneak in through the back door of the Community Center, then hide inside the building and lay in wait for the right time to...

The twelve-year-old girl who cried out for Lauren's help had barely survived a horrific experience that would dismantle someone who didn't have the support it took to heal. Shawn had managed to piece her life back together. Unfortunately, Lauren still felt the aftereffects.

Disoriented from the recurring nightmare, a chill from the master bedroom rendered Lauren numb. A red lace gown clung to her petite frame, wet from the perspiration that peppered her golden skin. She wrapped trembling arms about her midriff, but they provided no comfort. Lauren had watched Shawn's ordeal in excruciating detail through the sliver pane of glass the steel door offered.

"Help me," the girl screamed, but the man wrapped his thick fingers around her throat and cutting off any further speech.

This time in her nightmare, tornado sirens had roared loud enough to shatter glass windows and pierce eardrums. A howling wind swept through the building as the steel bars finally receded, and the evil man disappeared, leaving a world of sadness and torment behind.

Lauren scanned the dark bedroom, panting as her heart hammered against her chest causing an ache that wouldn't subside anytime soon. The guilt threatened to swallow her whole. She had allowed fear of someone else to control her actions, making her less mindful of following proper procedures. Now, thirteen years later, she sat on her bed reliving an experience that had been all consuming to the point she had been forced to seek medical help.

Lauren lowered her head, then took several deep breaths, watching her chest slowly rise and fall in efforts to create a steady breathing pattern.

Though the siren in her dream had silenced when she opened her eyes, some type of siren was still going strong on this side of Lauren's waking nightmare.

"What is that noise?" she whispered, and her voice seemed to disappear into corners of the master bedroom.

She focused on the digital clock on the nightstand, then shifted from the warmth under the comforter, her heart hammering in her chest all over again. When she stepped a few feet, the chilling grip of the dream loosened, and the cause for the blaring sound became that much clearer in her mind. At nearly three in the morning someone's car alarm was wailing louder than a Jessye Norman opera performance.

Lauren shivered as another chill raced through her body the moment her feet absorbed the coolness of the mahogany floor. Snatching a red satin robe from its home on the arm of a pewter suede wingback chair, she wrapped it around her body before rushing down the winding staircase and straight to the living room window. By the time she peered out of the vertical blinds, a few answering chirps had caused the noise to come to a complete stop.

She let out a heavy sigh, realizing that sleep wouldn't revisit her so soon after such an adrenaline rush. Normally the pills would keep her in a restful state through the entire night— no matter what happened in this corner of the world.

So, what's different this time?

Something was off, and her subconscious finally registered a particular issue with startling clarity. Xavier. Why didn't she wake him before venturing down to check things out for herself? Why hadn't he comforted her when she woke up shrieking from a horror that no longer existed?

The empty feel of the Tudor home they owned on the south side of Chicago, in the Beverly neighborhood, enveloped her like several layers of fog descending over Lake Michigan. Her husband's Cadillac Escalade wasn't in the driveway parked next to the White Lexus truck he'd bought her as a "just because" gift when she had been named as one of Chicago's Leading Hair Stylists in Essence Magazine.

She tried to shake off the feeling of melancholy which settled in as she made her way through the dark house, thinking that maybe she somehow misinterpreted things.

"Oh, my Lord," she whispered as a shocking reality set in. "Maybe that alarm was from his truck, and the damn thieves got away with it."

That had to be the only explanation for him to be missing in action. Since more DEA agents had been sent to Chicago, undercover work by local police was at a minimum. Xavier would have told Lauren of any new assignments.

Lauren climbed the stairs to the upper level, ran the length of the hallway, passing a red bamboo floor vase and causing it to shake from her efforts.

"Xavier! Xavier, wake up," Lauren yelled, bursting into the master bedroom. She flipped the light switch and froze; placing her hands on hips that her husband said would cause a blind man to regain his sight and dance a grateful jig. Evidently, that blind man had a better chance of seeing them right now than her husband would.

"Where the hell is he?"

Lauren's gaze swept the area, taking in the king-sized black canopy poster bed with two sheer drapes cascading down evenly on both sides.

Then her fingers tipped the dimmer. Her eyesight quickly adjusted to the bright light illuminating a room designed in shades of ruby red and Charleston gray—colors that spoke to a blend of the couple's taste.

Only Lauren's side of the bed showed signs of recent use. Xavier's was as silky smooth, just as it had been the morning before. Even the scent of Edge Shave gel was barely discernable.

She massaged her temples, allowing several scenarios to run through her mind. Her husband, a Narc with the Chicago Police Department, had been involved with the kind of cases that put him in the same vicinity with high-level drug dealers, managing confidential informants, and the type of surveillance that had made his career a sometimes-dangerous engagement. Nothing she was aware of would cause him to disappear without a word. And he certainly hadn't seemed worried about anything earlier that evening. Her body tingled with the sweet memories.

Xavier had touched, teased, and tongued every part of her soul along with every inch of her buttercream skin in the shower just hours ago. Her body had trembled and convulsed, as he drove her to the point that was completely out of control. He had perfected the craft of making Lauren experience the ultimate orgasmic euphoria. Their lovemaking now was as good as their wedding night had been a little over nine years ago. Only better. Coupled with the fact that he was also loving, caring, and an excellent provider, made her the happiest woman on the south side of Chicago, if not the world.

A smile crept across her face remembering that afterward, they had spooned and fell asleep in each other's arms. She ran her fingers through wavy shoulder-length hair, frowning as she tried to recall a fuzzier time, thinking; *I thought that's what happened?*

The smile disappeared the moment she tried putting the pieces together, and something didn't fit. Needless to say, no matter how much sleep was lacking and how much she needed to be on point to do an early morning favor for a last-minute client, she was too wired to put her head back on the pillow.

Lauren Carter wasn't sure if she should be pissed off at Xavier for being left alone or concerned because he wasn't in the place he was supposed to be.

"Where the hell is my husband?"

Chapter Two

Fueled by anger, Lauren rocketed from the entryway of the master bedroom to the nightstand where her cell phone rested. She snatched the iPhone from the charging cradle so fast that tiny beads emptied from a little orange bottle of sleeping pills and tap-danced across the wooden floor.

"Damn it." She dropped to her knees scrambling to retrieve what had become a nightly crutch for the past thirteen years. Frustrated, she jabbed her finger into the home-button and snapped, "Call Xavier," engaging the phone's auto-dial feature.

Lauren continued the frantic search for the rest of those magic pills while the phone connected her to the only number she could use to reach him. A number that had been drilled into her since day one. And she heeded that directive. But finding him was only one part of her concern. Her dependency on Ambien happened gradually over the years, and Dr. Harden had been steadily trying to wean her off. Now she was taking more than the doctor prescribed. Asking for another refill so soon would be completely suspect and out of the question.

Hi. You've reached Xavier Carter—

"Oh hell no." Lauren disconnected and dialed right back.

She spotted what she hoped was the last of the pills at the foot of the bed, blew on it, and dropped it in the cylindrical bottle, tightly fastened it, and gently placed it on the nightstand.

"Hi baby," Xavier answered on the second ring.

"Don't 'hi baby' me. Where the hell are you?" Lauren snapped.

That abnormal chill hit her again, and she walked to the marble bureau to find something clean and much drier to wear.

"What's wrong?" he asked, concern etched in his tone. "I can hear it in your voice."

"What? You can hear that I'm pissed? Let's give this man a gold star," she snarled, maneuvering around the armoire to get into the master bathroom to wash off. "Where are you? Don't make me ask again."

"I'm in the Crown Vic," he replied smoothly. Almost *too smoothly*. "I know you can hear the police scanner."

"What's your point, Xavier?" she huffed, still not placated by the answer while placing her focus on the bathroom mirror. She needed to wash off not only the perspiration but the memories as well.

"I'm at work," he said in a calm voice that only served to piss her off even more. "I told you before we went to bed last night that I had to follow up on a lead."

"No, you didn't. I wouldn't have forgotten something like that."

"Baby, I *told* you," Xavier responded in that soothing manner reserved for times when she was making a big deal out of nothing. "Maybe your mind's fuzzy after our rendezvous between the sheets, or did you forget that too?"

Lauren sucked her teeth at his blatant attempt to sidetrack the issue. "Whatever. Like I said, you didn't tell me."

"For argument's sake, let's say I forgot and for that I'm sorry." Xavier paused, waiting for Lauren to say something. When she didn't, he asked, "Now are you going to tell me what's wrong? It's not like you to wake up in the middle of the night."

She almost said, "How would you know?" as if her subconscious mind was planting the idea that this was not the first time.

Lauren snatched a face cloth from the gold bath ring, dampened it and dabbed her face, neck, and chest with cool water, then used another towel to pat herself dry. She wondered if she should mention the dream, but knowing that if she did, an ongoing argument would follow.

"I thought you took your meds?"

She opened her mouth to answer that he had been the one to bring water and the pills to her every night.

"Lauren, are you there?"

Her anger was quickly replaced with apprehension. Xavier had been adamant about Lauren seeking professional help for as long as she could remember. She wouldn't hear of it.

She already had a solution. Lauren figured if she could sleep soundly through the night, then that would make the dreams go away.

"I had another nightmare," she confessed, sliding her arms into a blue sleep shirt, then perching on the edge of the Jacuzzi. "I woke up, and you weren't here."

* * *

Xavier missed the overly confident woman he met in the barbershop. The Lauren who wasn't tainted by sins of something that had been out of her control. He wanted *her* back. Xavier closed his eyes while she unburdened her soul. He envisioned the "thick in all the right places" carefree woman he fell in love with. At that moment, the fragrance of her hair, coconut mixed with vanilla wafted through his nostrils. He smiled behind closed lids, remembering how Lauren lit into him about something he believed to be fake.

"Your eyes are beautiful."

"Thank you."

"Are those contacts?"

"What did you just ask me?" She flipped, swinging the barber chair around. "My eyes are natural, brother. Do you need to take a closer look?"

He didn't know. They matched her strawberry blonde hair. He chuckled at the memory, but he definitely had wanted a closer look— at all of her.

* * *

"Xavier, are you listening to me?"

"I'm sorry, babe," he said, and this time the regret in his tone was unmistakable. "You haven't had one of those dreams in a while."

She released a heavy sigh. "I don't know why this keeps haunting me after all this time. It's been thirteen years."

"Because you still blame yourself for what happened. You have to let yourself off the hook," Xavier urged. "It wasn't your fault."

Lauren traced the grout in the tile with a perfectly polished red toenail, "But I don't understand why the guilt is still there."

That evening thirteen years ago, she had been so worried about her boyfriend being upset that she neglected to follow procedure. The last thing she was required to do was make sure that all exit doors were locked, and no one was hiding in the bathroom stalls or anywhere else. Teenagers would do that to have a place make out, but she never feared a stranger lurking. A man who'd been waiting for the perfect opportunity to prey on one of the teens who came to the place for a haven after school which provided tutoring, and counseling. How wrong she had been.

"You are not your mistakes bab—"

"Shawn's foster mother was never on time," she whispered leaning in to turn on the water, opting for a bath since that provided only temporary relief. "Not Ms. Ida, but the previous foster parent." Xavier had heard it all before.

Marcus, Lauren's boyfriend, had been thirty minutes late for work the day before. They'd fought the moment she slid into the passenger seat. He'd slapped her so hard that her jaw shifted, and she saw stars.

Lauren caressed her left cheek at that ugly memory. Her cheekbone and lips suffered the consequences of that blow, leaving her with a crooked smile for a long while. She squeezed her eyes shut and swallowed hard, trying to wipe the visual of his cruelty from her. A man had never hit her before, not even her father who had found other ways to discipline her. Then Marcus stuck his index finger in her temple so hard that a headache sprang to life. He told her she'd better not *ever* have him waiting again or else he'd beat her ass, then leave her stranded.

She had just moved from New York and didn't know her way around Chicago. But that wasn't any excuse. As a New Yorker, she knew the ins and outs of public transportation. Chicago should be no different. She was so wrapped up in *him*, and his *ride*, and his *money*, and his *needs* that she couldn't think straight. Lauren's parents had her on such a short leash as a teenager; she couldn't do anything without one of them. The taste of freedom made Lauren lose her head—and her mind.

"I was so stupid back then," she admitted, meaning that day and those, which followed, as the abuse from Marcus became a recurring thing. All it took was that one time, and he felt entitled to hit her whenever he felt the urge—— which was too often for Lauren's taste.

"Stop saying that," he warned, and the scanner crackled in the background. "You were never stupid. I hate when you talk down about yourself."

She shifted on the edge of the tub, trying to hold back tears.

"We've all made bad choices when we were younger," Xavier said sincerely. "I know I've made quite a few."

Lauren wiped away the tears that fell but was unable to agree.

"Shawn doesn't blame you, and it's time for you to stop blaming yourself. She's like family."

She'd lost count the number of times Shawn had been to their home over the years. "You're right," Lauren responded, her gaze focused on the water filling the tub.

Lauren was quiet for a moment, picturing the vulnerable young girl Shawn was when she first came to the Thompson Center, instead of the fierce young woman she had become.

"But every time I have that dream, it takes me right back to that place and time."

"That's why you need to talk to somebody about it."

"Not this again." Lauren sighed, anger flaring. "I told you I'm good. I don't need to see a damn psychiatrist. I'm not crazy."

"Therapist, Lauren," he corrected.

"Whatever," she shot back. "Same thing."

Silence filled the air for a few moments.

"I can go with you if it'll make it easier."

She took a calming breath. "Hear me clearly, Xavier. I don't *want* or *need* to see a head doctor. You got it?"

"Says the woman who's been having nightmares for years," he countered. She had no comeback for that. "What happened to Shawn affected you too."

Lauren stomped her foot so hard; she nearly slipped into the tub.

"So, who do you think you are, Dr. Phil?"

This constant battle had her insides boiling like she'd ingested an entire bottle of Tabasco sauce. "I'm the one who left her alone after hours. I'm the one who didn't check the doors." She turned off the water, then stormed out of the bathroom, abandoning the whole idea of a bath. Why was he so ready to have the doctor certify her as crazy and put her on all kinds of heavier medication?

She pulled the duvet back on Xavier's side of the bed and laid down. "I don't need a head doctor telling me what I already know. All I need is sleep."

"Don't get an attitude with me, Lauren," he snapped. "All I'm saying is—"

"Nothing. I gotta get some sleep."

"Damn baby. It's like that?"

"Yep, it's *exactly* like that," she shot back, and Lauren disconnected the call.

Chapter Three

Xavier pulled the phone away from his ear and stared at it; unable to believe his wife had hung up on him. The series of beeps confirmed the abrupt disconnection of the call, so whether he couldn't believe it or not, the truth was——she had.

He flipped off the police scanner sitting on the bookcase, then shook his head. He returned the cell phone to the secret desk compartment in the study of the home he shared with Patricia, his wife of eighteen years and their fifteen-year-old son, Xavier Junior.

Xavier swept all concerns aside at the unexpected exchange, reclined in the leather office chair, folded his hands behind his head, then propped his feet on top of the smooth wooden surface of the desk before closing his eyes. Xavier's six-foot-five, dark chocolate, muscular frame contoured to the shape of the chair as the tension he didn't realize had coiled through him, finally eased.

With those pills securely in her system, he never worried about Lauren catching on that he rarely shared their bed overnight. He was there long before she closed her eyes, then left the moment that even breathing set in. Although the reason behind her Ambien habit was disturbing, it had worked in his favor for nine years. Usually, by the time she awakened from those nightmares, he was back in place on the other side of the bed.

What was so different about tonight?

He closed his eyes, envisioning what would happen if his worlds collided. Patricia would leave him and then he would rarely see his son. Lauren would pack up and go back to New York as she had threatened to do when she gave him that world-shattering ultimatum. The irreversible hurt and damage he would bring to the two women he loved would be unbearable.

Sometimes he wondered what he could have done differently, but none of the scenarios included having both women he loved so much. And he couldn't see that in his future. So, the path he'd taken was one he had to live with. They did too. Although neither of them were aware they shared a husband with another woman. He aimed to keep it that way forever.

The soft touch of silky hands and the scent of cherry blossoms stirred him from a nap of what seemed only minutes but might have been much longer. The feel and smell were both things he'd enjoyed since he first laid eyes on her during an Omega Psi Phi Step Show at Fisk University twenty years ago.

Xavier was in the middle of a routine with his line brothers when the chocolate beauty grabbed his attention. His eyes connected with hers the one-time Patricia glanced up from a book to sweep a loose strand of hair behind her ear. Her eyes smiled at him, causing Xavier to miss a step, and his brothers to give him a hard glare. Patricia grinned and returned to reading, unbothered by the controlled chaos of everything around her— student chatter, feet slamming against the bleachers, cheers of students encouraging the frat brothers. Xavier was intrigued. Women went out of their way to get— and keep — his attention, but not her.

After the show, he searched, but couldn't find her in the crowd. He waited outside of Jubilee Hall since that was the freshman residence hall for women. That had to be the only reason he had never seen her beautiful face before. He had no luck, so he headed back to Livingstone Hall.

Along the way to his dorm, the glowing lights from the library burned like the moon in the dark sky. On a Friday night, only someone who was serious about their studies would be there instead of partying with everyone else. Glancing down at his watch, he took off running. The library closed in fifteen minutes.

Patricia was packing up her things when he slid through the glass doors. He wiped the sweat from his hairline, took a deep breath, then approached the brown skinned beauty. Xavier had no idea then that she was the future Mrs. Carter, a woman who would capture his heart with beauty, class, and brilliance. She didn't make things easy for him as other girls did, and he loved the challenge. Patricia was a lady in every sense. She even refused to sleep with him. Xavier had to choose her, and only her. And that worked for years, until… Lauren.

Xavier shifted his head on the headrest, nuzzled his nose on the back of Patricia's manicured hand and gently pressed his lips against the tip of her fingers.

"Hey, my beautiful Patty," he whispered, an endearment of sorts.

She tugged his earlobe slightly where he used to wear a princess-cut diamond earring that eventually became her engagement ring. One of Xavier's frat brothers worked for a carpenter. Xavier paid him to carve a replica of a ring Patricia always fawned over when they passed by Rogers & Hollands Jewelers in the mall. He set it with the diamond from his earring. A beautiful Indian Rosewood ring she loved and wore until this very day, even though Xavier upgraded her. "You spending the night down here?"

"Not at all. I received a work-related call and didn't want to disturb you, so I came down here."

Her thinly arched eyebrows drew in. "Really? Jason said he'd been ringing your phone non-stop for the past twenty minutes."

Jason was his partner and friend of fourteen years, and if he was going through all channels to get to Xavier, then something was definitely wrong—and his little lie wasn't going to cover him.

"He couldn't reach you," she added peering at him as she handed him the cordless phone. "That's what woke me up."

"Thank you, baby. I must have fallen asleep." Xavier swung his legs around to the side of the desk; the chair swiveled, landing him in an upright position. He covered the receiver and said, "I won't be long."

Patricia smiled as those wide shapely hips swayed slowly on the way out. "I sure hope not."

She pulled the door closed behind her, letting the unspoken seduction and expectation carry its weight.

* * *

Xavier went to the door, listening for Patricia to reach the top of the stairs, and the master bedroom door to shut.

"I *know* you know better than to call me at the crib," he growled into the receiver. "I'll call you right back on my cell."

Xavier disconnected the call, feeling almost as furious as Lauren had sounded earlier. He switched on his cell, and it immediately blew up with notices of recent calls and text messages from his partner. Jason picked up on half a ring, and Xavier said, "This better be good."

"Man, get your ass out here," Jason commanded, undeterred by Xavier's angry vibe. "Ain't nobody got time for your shenanigans. We got work to do."

Xavier tensed, pulling the phone away from his ear to check the time. "Wait … what?"

"Throw your drawers on— clean ones— and let's go. I'm outside."

Evidently, a night of passionate lovemaking and cuddling with the woman he'd been married to for eighteen years was not on the agenda. "Give me five minutes. I'll be right out."

"You got two."

Xavier ran upstairs into the master suite, pulled off his lounge pants and slipped into a pair of black jeans, a long sleeve black fitted shirt, and stepped into a pair of black steel toe work boots.

"Tonight's the night," he said staring at his beautiful wife whose radiant sable skin matched his own. Her expression transformed from joyful to one of disappointment, something he'd seen too much of lately.

While strapping on a bulletproof vest, Patricia finally eased off the bed, reached into the nightstand drawer and retrieved the undercover badge and ID holder. She paused for a moment, staring at his wedding band resting in the crystal dish inside the drawer. She still wasn't used to not seeing it on his finger. He'd explained that early on in their marriage that he couldn't wear it to work. Closing the drawer, she sauntered over to where he stood, went up on her tippy toes and slid the beaded silver chain over his head and tucked it in his shirt.

"You'd better come back to me, Detective Carter," she warned, smoothing his shirt over the badge.

"Always." His arms went around her thick waist, resting his fingertips on her ample bottom. Then he lowered to kiss her on the forehead. He lifted her chin so he could gaze into her deep-set cocoa eyes. "I will always come back to you. Believe that."

Xavier left her warmth, walked to the closet and extracted a black leather shoulder holster. Patricia adjusted the straps across his broad shoulders and chest. He slid the service weapon in the holder that rested along his torso, then she grabbed his waist-length black leather jacket and held it so he could slide his arms inside. This ritual was almost a seduction in itself if the reason hadn't been so deadly.

She playfully slapped his ass and gave him a frisky grin before turning to make her way back to their bed. She made the first few steps, he reached out to grab her hand and pulled her closer.

"I love you."

Xavier embraced her, enjoying the soft feel of her body against his. He kissed the tip of her nose, then her lips. "I'll see you later."

"I'll be waiting."

* * *

Xavier jogged down the curved staircase and was out the door. He hopped in an unmarked midnight blue Chevy Suburban parked in the driveway where Jason awaited.

"What's up, Jay?" They gave each other their customary fist bump.

"Hey. Did you kiss *my* wife and son goodbye?" Jason teased, a smirk on his thin lips.

"Whatever man," Xavier said, waving him off as he buckled up. "I told you about that shit."

"I'm just checking dude," he replied, laughing as he made a left turn out of the driveway. "I got to make sure my wife and kid are okay since fate's got you looking after them instead of me. What's up with that?"

"Keep cracking jokes man, and it's gonna be a 1-8-7 on an undercover cop," he warned. "For real, executed by yours truly."

Jason gave him the side eye. "Look who's Mr. Sensitive tonight. What's your problem?"

Xavier let out a long, slow breath. "Man, Lauren called me at the crack of dawn wanting to know where I was."

"Yikes."

"I thought Patty heard the phone ring, so I let the call go to voicemail, then I had to dash downstairs to my office before she called back."

Jason raised an eyebrow, before making a right turn onto the Dan Ryan Expressway and flooring it. "I thought you said Lauren was a sound sleeper?"

"She usually is."

Jason took his focus off the road and put it on Xavier for a moment. "She's still taking those sleeping pills, right?"

"Yeah, man." Xavier grimaced at the memory of that heated conversation with Lauren. "Turns out she's still having crazy dreams about that incident from gazillion years ago," he said dryly. "If she'd get therapy like I told her, she wouldn't be having these problems. She thinks those sleeping pills are a cure, but they aren't."

"They must be doing something," Jason commented, checking the side mirror. "This is the first time you've said something like this has happened."

"True, but they can't replace speaking with someone who specializes in her kind of situation."

"Hold up," Jason said, taking another quick glance at Xavier. "Who is she getting the pills from then?"

"Her primary doctor." Xavier shrugged. "I don't know what story Lauren told her, but she's been filling them for years."

"Damn dude, is that legal?"

"Apparently so." Xavier adjusted the tuner on the police scanner to hear the call without static interference. "But in the meantime, she expects me to be her savior when her version of "therapy" falls through."

"Well, that's what you sign up for when you say I do..." Jason frowned. "And aw, that's right, you said that twice— so that's I do, and I do."

"Your ass is on a roll tonight, I see." Xavier pointed out. "Sandy must've broken you off a little something-something before you left home, huh?"

"Don't be mad at me, bruh," he said, popping his collar. "This sexy white chocolate has only one wife to please and not nearly the high blood pressure you signed up for." Jason winked one crystal-blue eye, flexing his boulder-sized biceps. "More wives..."

"Mo problems. Whatever dude."

"So, what did you tell her?" Jason asked as he swiftly maneuvered into the local lanes and whizzed past the few cars.

Xavier shrugged, then put his focus on the traffic moving at a much slower pace than they were. "I told her I had to work."

"Well, for once you didn't lie," Jason teased. "It must be work trying to keep two women happy and clueless."

Lies. He'd been leading this double-life long enough to know they were necessary. The less his wives knew, the easier his life became.

Unfortunately, some of the new cases thrown their way were the high-profile types. The kind that the media sniffed around, vying to be first on the scene and the first to report.

Jason had requested a transfer from the Twenty-First District when his first partner, Scott, was killed in the middle of a drug bust. Though Sergeant Armstrong tried to deter Jason from leaving, his request was granted, but not before a new trainee was dropped in his lap. Though he wasn't happy about the situation, Jason took an eager young Detective Carter under his wing. He was impressed by Xavier's sharpness in the field and his quick ability to assess situations. After six months of training, Jason had bonded with Xavier so much so that he rescinded his request to transfer.

Xavier's street savvy coupled with Jason's experience rocketed the duo to the head of their unit. Fourteen years later, they were still dismantling cases that no one else could, drawing the jealous ire of some officers who had been working similar cases with less than stellar results. Now they had to watch their backs because Xavier and Jason believed that two detectives in their unit might be dirty. That would cause a major scandal. And as one of the lead investigators on the cases that put kingpins and distributors in prison, staying off the news was getting harder every day.

Available on Amazon/Kindle Unlimited

Excerpt of
Domino Effect by Gisele Marie

(Coming Soon)

Present Day

"I can't believe you would mess with her. Out of all the shit I've been through with you, why would it be okay to cheat on me?" an emotionally charged Blaine screamed at the top of her lungs, as anger dominated her body and simultaneously caused anxiety tremors. Feeling her bangle slip off her wrist, Blaine knew her inability to stay in control was slipping through her fingers.

I'd kill them both if I could right now, with no regrets.

"What are you looking at? Both of you ruined my life. I hate you," Alyssa spat with a mixture of mucus and tears between each word.

Blaine began to count to ten in her head. If Alyssa were in arm's length when her count concluded, jail would be home for the night. Before she could count to five, Alyssa grabbed her purse and stumbled out the front door. Turning to face Javier, he stood next to her with closed eyes and his arms resting on the top of his head. Blaine could only blame herself. Falling in love with the wrong man always came with complications, even if he claimed to be a changed man.

Javier firmly gripped Blaine by the forearm, then escorted her to the back door of the lounge. "Let's go." Removing his hand, Blaine swiftly walked to the passenger side of Javier's Challenger.

After flopping her body into the front seat, Blaine tried to express her pain and frustration through her tears. "Javier, I'm not understanding how you think it's ok to cheat on me. We been through so much shit in the last couple of years, why this? Why now?"

"I told you, Alyssa was cool. The shit just happened. Sometimes, I don't think you understand why people don't care to be around you. It's always ok for you to do some shit, but other people gotta be fucking perfect for your ass and you far from it. You didn't have a problem fucking me before I married my wife and during my marriage."

For the first time, Blaine was speechless. Instead of expressing random feelings, she'd wait until they arrived home. That would ensure she had his undivided attention, and it gave her time to make a final decision about which direction their future headed.

Thirty minutes later, Javier pulled into their apartment complex. He parked in their assigned spot and shut off the car. Blaine removed her seatbelt and intertwined her fingers, then turned and leaned her back against the door, giving Javier all of her attention. He sluggishly dragged his hands down his face. Nine years his senior, Blaine hoped that someday he would understand her and love her for the flaws she possessed.

Looking in her direction, Javier broke the silence first. "Babe, I have to own up to what I did. I'm sorry I hurt you and cheated. There's no excuse," he confessed, gazing directly into her eyes.

"Javier, I love you, but I can't do this. My ex-boyfriend cheated, and I promised myself I wouldn't settle for being treated how someone else sees fit. You know you—"

Boom!

Her words cut off as their car slammed into the lobby of the building; the impact forcefully whipped Blaine's head into the dashboard. Glass projected across the interior of the vehicle, as blood oozed from the side of Javier's head. The seatbelt prevented him from going through the windshield, but Blaine was feeling dizzy and partially incoherent. Scanning the area for help, Javier pulled at the door handle, but his door was jammed and wouldn't open no matter how hard he tried.

Eyes glazed and ringing in her ears, Blaine saw a shadowy figure walking toward the car. Feeling her conscious slipping, Blaine called Javier with a hoarse voice, but the active fire alarm drowned her words. The shadow was now replaced by a person dressed in all black who stood at the shattered window on the passenger's side. Blaine tried, but she couldn't make out any features. The individual slowly squatted just before she'd gone completely unconscious...

"Damn, you're still breathing. I'll try again and do better next time."

Website: www.AuthorGiseleMarie.com
Facebook: Author Gisele Marie
Instagram: authorgiselemarie
Twitter: @authorgiselemarie

Also by London St. Charles

The Husband We Share
Sugarcoated Deception

ANTHOLOGIES

Sugar
Sugar & Spice Cookbook
Just One Kiss

COMING LATER 2019

Deadly Deception
Sixty Days of Pleasure
Kings of the Castle